Cover illustration: Soviet surface to air (SAM) missile SA–8. NATO code name, Gecko. Slant range 8.5 miles. Infra-red homing. Warhead weight 105 lbs (with proximity fuse). Fired in pairs to defeat electronic counter measures; typical interception speed is Mach 1.5.

The six-wheeled amphibious transporter is based on components of the ZIL–E167 truck. A central tyre pressure regulation system is fitted and the vehicle is sealed for use in NBC environments. Usually employed well forward, the lack of armour has proved a handicap, the radar group in particular being vulnerable to damage by shell fragments. (A tracked armoured carrier is under development.)

Eight reload rounds are carried; when they have been used it is necessary for the crew to ballast the vehicle before attempting river crossings. The 12.7mm DShK machine gun, shown on the example is a local modification.

HUNTER-KILLER
James Rouch

NEW ENGLISH LIBRARY/TIMES MIRROR

For Lily and Bill Mellor

A New English Library Original Publication, 1981

First NEL Paperback Edition March 1981

NEL Books are published by
New English Library Limited,
Barnard's Inn, Holborn,
London, EC1N 2JR.

Made and printed in Great Britain by
Hunt Barnard Printing Ltd., Aylesbury, Bucks.

0 450 05010 6

'As I see it, World War Three will be fought in two places; in Western Europe, and on and under every damned inch of ocean around the globe.'

Admiral Harvey J. Harrison, US Navy (Retired), in an off-the-record conversation before a televised debate on armament spending, June 1978.

The Atlantic. Aircraft from the USS Carl Vinson, *lead ship of the nuclear powered task force commanded by Admiral Howard Murray, have made their second 'kill' in three days, bringing to four the number of Soviet submarines destroyed by the Force in as many weeks. NATO sources have expressed confidence that the threat to the convoy routes is steadily diminishing. Merchant shipping losses in the last quarter were down by 46 per cent, to 789,000 tons for that theatre.*

The Mediterranean. The Palestinian gunboat, Black September *(ex-Soviet Poluchat class patrol boat) has been sunk by the Israeli helicopter/missile craft* Aliya.

A mixed force of British and American destroyers has sunk the Soviet fleet replenishment ship Boris Chilikin *(23,00 tons) and driven aground or damaged three Mirka class frigates off Kinaros, at the entrance to the Aegean Sea. HMS* Birmingham *and USS* Dewey *suffered some damage in the night engagement, but are remaining on station.*

The Pacific. Rescue and decontamination parties are now satisfied they have located all of the survivors aboard the USS Nimitz. *Rough weather has prevented the transfer of the last of the casualties to the hospital ship* Sanctuary, *but a volunteer medical team has* established facilities aboard the carrier. With 140 feet of the bow and its island superstructure gone and the bodies of a thousand crew members still on board, it is thought likely, though the Navy Department has issued no statement as yet, that the ship will eventually be sunk as a war grave. The warhead that inflicted the damage, killing 50 per cent of the 6,328 strong complement, is estimated at 5Kt.

The North Sea/Baltic Approaches/Baltic. In the past week, five new hulls have been launched from the Soviet naval shipyards at Leningrad, and four warships have completed fitting-out, including a Kresta class cruiser. Three refitted destroyers and six new frigates have joined the squadrons working-up off the coast of Poland.

Increased radio activity and the ships' deployment has been taken by the NATO Intelligence Staffs as an indication that the Russians may shortly attempt a breakout into the North Sea. If successful this would totally alter the balance of power in the area, and seriously threaten the resupply of NATO ground forces in the Zone.

There is intense diplomatic activity between Stockholm and Moscow, and it is thought likely that the Russians are bringing pressure to bear on Sweden to gain rights of passage for Warsaw Pact combat vessels through her territorial waters. If this is granted, then the Soviet ships will be able to avoid the extensive NATO minefields in the Kattegat. Strenuous efforts to counter the Russian move are being made by Western diplomats, who fear that such a concession could be the forerunner of an agreement between the two countries that would virtually take Sweden into the Soviet camp.

ONE

Flames were coming from the port inner engine of the giant Ilyshin military transport. As the aircraft banked steeply towards the cover of broken cloud below, the feather-edged yellow streamer of fire spread along the high-set wing to its root. It seared away the banded green and brown camouflage paint and its furnace heat buckled the thin alloy skin of the fuselage. The blazing two-shaft turbofan suddenly broke from its pylon and whirled into space, trailing a ribbon of blue smoke.

For an instant a bank of cloud hid the aircraft from sight, then as it emerged into clear sky once more, it was wracked by an internal explosion that littered the air with anonymous debris. Huge sheets of ragged metal were caught and tossed by the slip-stream. The nose of the Ilyshin dropped sharply as it began its last, uncontrolled descent.

There followed a second, more violent explosion that tore the flame-enveloped wing from the transport, and it rolled on to its back and began to break up as it went into a steep dive. A moment before the clouds hid it again, the rear cargo doors burst open and the sky was seeded with the burning fragments of its palletised load and the tumbling bodies of its handling crew.

'Don't get fucking excited. It's not a real-time transmission. The general likes a few tapes of edited highlights played when things are a little slack.'

Major Revell didn't need to look away from the big screen and the operations room spread out below to know that it

7

was Ol' Foul Mouth who stood behind him on the balcony. The dramatic scenes of the recording had already been replaced with grid, continent outline and vari-coloured coded symbols of the status chart as he turned from the rail. 'When do I get my command, Colonel?'

'Shit, you still rumbling on about that?' Colonel Lippincott shied the half-inch stub of pencil into a waste basket on the floor below and xylophoned his teeth with a fresh one, before testing its composition with a crunching bite. 'Come with me, I'll explain how it is.'

Led at a fast pace half the length of the underground complex, Revell had no chance to repeat his question, as both keeping up and the narrowness of some passageways prevented him from putting it again.

'Well?' Lippincott threw open a rivet-studded steel door to reveal a small room not more than ten by ten. The bare, rough hewn walls of natural rock were relieved at intervals by unframed rectangles of startlingly daubed canvas. 'So tell me, what d'yer think?'

Not certain what it was he was supposed to comment on, Revell played safe. 'It isn't what I was expecting.'

'You can bet your fucking arse it isn't. You know, I got better than ninety-five square feet here. There's a two-star general down the corridor apiece who ain't got half that, and he has to share with a couple of buckets and a mini-mop. How d'yer like the paintings?' He didn't give Revell a chance to reply. 'Did them myself. Kinda hobby of mine.'

Grateful to have been spared the need to conjure up what could only have been an unconvincing 'very nice', Revell sat on the canvas sling of the metal-framed chair he was waved to, and waited for Ol' Foul Mouth to settle in the swivelling bucket-style seat on the other side of the wide polished desk that dominated the artificially lit room.

'My one little luxury.' Lippincott ran his hand over the beautifully waxed wood. 'Had to slip a couple of fifties to a horse-faced master sergeant to get it in, but I feel happier with it down here, tucked away nice and safe.'

'There must be a lot of German civvies up above who'd like to feel the same about themselves.'

'Shit, they're safe enough.' Lippincott jerked his thumb towards the rock ceiling. 'They're a good twenty of their crappy kilometres from the Zone. Unless the Commies start breaking the rules again, and sling a few nukes around outside of it, they're safe. Give or take a spot of shitty fallout, that is.'

'What about my command?' Revell was growing impatient with the drawn-out preliminaries.

Taking a file from the neat stack barely lining the bottom of a wire basket, Lippincott flicked it open and smoothed the top sheet of crisp white paper. 'Before we get to that, I got the Staff verdict on that little job you did for me.'

'Verdict?' There'd been no special emphasis on the word, but it warned Revell to be on his guard.

'That's what I fucking said. Seems the good citizens of Frankfurt got their knickers a mite twisted over that . . . shall we call it "adventure", of yours.' The colonel's finger found a particular line on the double spaced report. 'As I read it, seems like they could have forgiven you for scaring the crap out of them with that false Nuke alert while you flattened one of their showpiece industrial estates; but what stuck in their craw was coming back out of their shelters to find you'd done a hell of a demolition job on a key power station, and fucked-up who knows how many millions of man-hours of war effort.'

'I did the job I was given. My men destroyed the Ruskie armoured column . . .'

'Yeah, and that's probably what saved your hide, otherwise by now you'd be a shit-house cleaner, tenth class.'

'Are you telling me I don't get the Special Combat Company I was promised three months back, is that it?' Revell leant forward and the top back rail of his chair clanged against the stone. 'I've got just seven men, seven. A couple of the survivors from that other group we absorbed might be worth hanging on to, but that's it.' He included Andrea in the number, counting her among the men. Judging by her ability to take care of herself, there was no reason why he should do otherwise.

'Sit still. Hell, there ain't the room to get excited and start jumping about in here. OK, so that's how it is at the moment . . . now will you fucking sit, shut it, and listen . . . ' Lippincott forestalled the objections and protest he sensed coming. 'Jesus, you bastards with the combat commands think you're the only ones fighting this shitty war. All you got to fight is sneak-punching Russians; me, I've got to do battle with a dozen different cruddy Staff whizzkids every day. Every damned day. You know the latest bee they got in their swollen heads? Course you fucking don't. Private armies.'

A crudely secured extension vent, from the main air-conditioning trunk in the passageway, gave a sudden shudder and a tinny clatter of vibration at a distant impact and vomited a spoonful of fine dust that floated down to settle on the desk top. It had hardly touched before Lippincott was deftly brushing it to the floor with a soft yellow cloth he took, neatly folded, from a top drawer. Only when the oak surface was once again without blemish did he flap the residue from his shoulders and his stump-encasing sleeve.

'You any idea how many brigade, divisional, even army commanders are trying to grab the headlines by forming special units? It's a hell of a lot. Word has come down that it's got to stop. Too much dilution of effort is the reason given. Me, I reckon it's pressure from the guys running the Rangers and Commandos and the SAS. They don't want their thunder stolen.'

'So my new outfit gets its wings clipped even before it takes off.' The news wasn't a complete surprise to Revell. He'd been half expecting something like it.

'Yeah, but only clipped. A lot of others have been plucked, stuffed and cooked.' Closing the file, Lippincott replaced it, and took a second from a locked centre drawer. 'I got something else for you here, just to keep you ticking over. It's a toughy, but tailor-made for the size of your squad.' He paused a moment before going on. 'How you feel about starting a war?'

For a second Revell thought he must have misheard him. 'Damn it, Colonel, what have we got now? A two-hundred-mile wide no-man's-land running the length of Europe; ten million dead civvies, four times that number of refugees . . . what more do you want?'

'We want Sweden in the war, on our side. Finland could be forced into the Russian camp at any time, it's practically in it now. Like bloody Frog-land it's more fucking neutral to the Commies than it is to us. Shoots at us if we only look that way, and meantime supplies the Ruskies with everything from ice-breakers to bootlaces and pyjama cords. If Sweden comes in on our side it would give us a good base from which to try and get back into the Baltic. Command aren't too happy about it having become a Russian lake, and with the Finns having to worry about the Swedish army they wouldn't be able to spare men to help the Russians in Norway.'

'The country's armament industry would be useful, too.' The attractions of the possibility were obvious to Revell.

'That'd be a bonus.'

'How is the miracle going to be worked? The Swedes are firmly neutral, they've been treading very careful with the Russians.'

Lippincott smiled. 'The Ruskies are going to help us, but they don't know it yet. Come to that, they won't know until after they have. What's the weather like outside? I haven't been above ground for a week.'

To Revell the question seemed an irrelevance. 'Very cold, threatening snow. Why?'

'The weather boffins reckon all the little old ladies are being proved right at last. All those tactical nukes both sides have been so cheerfully chucking about inside the Zone have screwed the climate. Winter will be early this year, stay longer and bite a lot harder. Satellites tell us that the Russians are already having to do round-the-clock ice-breaking to keep Leningrad and the other northern Baltic ports and yards open. There's seven-tenths pack as far south as Gdansk and if they're going to get all the hardware their yards have been building or updating out into the Atlantic, then they'll have to be moving it real soon . . .'

'Where does my squad fit in, and how's Sweden going to be dragged in?'

'The Swedes have given the Commies the OK to make the passage to open sea through their territorial waters, so we lose our chance to hit them in the narrows of the Baltic approaches. Once they reach the Skaggerak and the North Sea they'll spread out, have more room to man-oeuvre, and altogether be a fucking tough target. Any we miss will be able to play havoc with either the Brits' oil-rigs or our convoy routes. Just when it begins to look like we got the measure of their subs, they're going to chuck surface units our way.' Spitting with machine-gun rapidity and accuracy, Lippincott sent fragments of soggy pencil wood into an ashtray. 'We're going to dump you and your men on a small island inside Swedish territorial waters, where the Russians will have to pass close. You'll be given enough firecrackers to scare the shit out of the Commies as they come racing out of the narrows between Sweden and the occupied Danish islands. If our Russian friends perform as per usual, they'll plaster the nearest Swedish territory with everything they've got. You should have a nice ringside seat for the first battle between the Commies and our newest ally.'

'And what if they're not so obliging?' The many prob-lems the thumbnail sketch of the mission presented crowded in upon Revell.

'If the Ruskies don't lash out, then you'll have a multiple warhead Lance missile to stir them into action yourself. Nothing that'll do them any real harm, but it should get the party going.' Swivelling back and forth in his chair, and chewing furiously, Lippincott waited for the major's reaction.

'My men will be on the nearest chunk of Sweden when the Russians open fire. I'd like to know just how much ordnance is likely to come our way. What's the size of the force that'll be making the breakout?'

'Can't be sure at this stage. You'll get provisional figures before you go, and we'll feed you updates once you're established.'

'What's the estimate? There must be a number flying around somewhere.'

'It's only a guess, but Staff are working on the assumption there'll be ten major units and thirty-plus destroyers, frigates and mine hunters as escorts. You'll only be going for the big stuff, cruisers and the like.'

'And what do we hit them with? The Swedes have a good radar net. If we're going to land undetected we have to be travelling light. Since when has NATO had a weapon with a decent range, the ability to resist jamming and get through a ship's close-in defences, with a warhead hefty enough to upset the captain of a fifteen thousand ton cruiser, that'll fit into a shoe box?'

'Shit, range won't matter much. The Ruskies will have to pass within four miles of the island, probably less. They ain't the best seamen in the war, they'll allow a healthy margin for navigation error. Those shits know that if they stick so much as a double thickness of battleship grey outside the limits, we'll hit it with everything we've got. We can get around jamming by using a weapon that's just point and fire. If it doesn't employ guidance then it can't be buggered by electronic countermeasures. As for getting past the ships' SAMs and radar directed gatlings, they'll be beaten by saturation tactics. Send twenty rockets at a target, don't matter if it's bristling with every type of flak, some of them are going to get through, especially in the minimal flight time we're envisaging.'

'That's not a description of any anti-shipping missile that I know of.'

'That's cause it's not. The British gunners who are going with you will have simple, lightweight, trailer-mounted versions of our standard 125mm multiple rocket launchers. The sort our artillery boys use all the time. Fucking clever, ain't it? The Ruskies will have planned for everything; mines, torpedoes, air-attacks, the lot, you name it they'll be ready for it. The one thing they won't be prepared for is for you to have a go at them from a direction they'll not be expecting with a weapon that's never been used that way before.'

A major drawback occurred to Revell. 'OK, it sounds smart, but even if they all get through to the target,

13

125mm rounds are going to do little more than skin damage to those big battlewagons. They'll shrug it off like so many flea bites and plough on.'

'We're one ahead of you. Going back a bit, one of our destroyers off 'Nam was on the receiving end of an accidental near miss from an air-launched missile one of our pilots let go by mistake. It was a Shrike I think, anyway, it had a fragmentation head and when it banged off right over our ship it took out all her radar, diced better than twenty of her crew and stopped the tub dead in the water. It was kept kinda quiet at the time. The babies you'll be taking have been fitted with similar heads. If just one of them bangs off over a Ruskie ship it'll be as good as poking the fucker's eyes out. Any Commie admiral should take that serious enough.'

'Maybe if we did enough damage we could force them to turn around, go back for repairs. That'd lock them up for the rest of the winter.'

'Don't start getting over-ambitious, Major. That's what the city fathers of Frankfurt were beefing about. Just do the job as it's given you. If you manage to knock them about, sufficient to soften them up for a reception by the Brit Navy when they reach open sea, good. But just remember, Copenhagen is not so far from there. At the moment the Ruskies are accepting the Danes' declaration of it being an open city: they've occupied it, but they ain't harmed it yet. You overdo things and that might change. We need the Free Danish Forces. No point in roping Sweden into the fight if we upset and maybe lose an established member of NATO in the process.'

'Alright, so let's asume it all goes according to plan, and the Commies and the Swedes start chucking ordnance at each other. What about my men? We'll be in the middle of the cauldron, and back-loading our equipment is not going to be easy. If we leave a load of NATO gear on the island it won't take the Swedes long to figure out that someone has been doing some stirring. Could rather spoil things.'

'Ain't that the truth. When you've done, you'll destroy

14

what you can't carry. It'll have to be done thorough, but it's a small price to pay for fucking up a Soviet fleet.'

'What about the men? Are you fitting them with self-destruct mechanisms?'

Coming from another man Lippincott might have seen humour in the question but not from Revell, strait-laced crud! 'The planning ain't got that far yet, but you'll be picked up as soon as the excitement dies down, or moves elsewhere. Sub, or chopper, or surface craft; we ain't sure yet.' He tidied the sheets of paper together. 'The rest you'll get at briefing before the "off". We've got to move real fast on this one. Met reckon the Commies will have to make a move inside the next eight days. I want you and your crowd kitted and on your way within twenty-four hours. Oh yeah, a last piece of good news. You won't be exactly making a landing on the island, leastways, not the way you mean, from the sea. I've arranged a little treat for you, you're going in by parachute.'

'The hell we are! Better find yourself another suicide squad. None of my men are trained, give it to the SAS or the Screaming Eagles. I'm beginning to think you snatched the mission from them in the first place.'

'Scared the shit out of you, have I?'

'No,' Revell kept the irritation out of his voice, but it took an effort. 'No, you just wasted my time.' He made to leave.

'OK, so I was only kidding, you're not actually making a drop. Well, not a real one.'

'You want to try explaining that piece of gobbledygook, or shall I keep heading for the door?'

'Ever seen parachute extraction?'

'Where a transport comes in low and slow with its rear doors open and chutes deploy to drag out a sled-mounted cargo? Sure, I've seen it . . . you want my men to go to war that way? Are you crazy, that's strictly hardware only.'

'They've refined it a bit . . .'

'What did they do, fit the sledge with springs so it can pogo back inside if it goes down in the wrong place?'

15

Again Lippincott sensed no light intent behind the remark. 'I'm telling you, it's OK. There'll be three pallets. One will carry the launchers, their ammunition and the demolition charges, along with most of the electronics gadgets you'll be taking. Another will have a generator, a small tractor for dispersing the launchers and moving your stores, and your support arms and ammunition. Number three will have a cabin that you'll all ride down in.'

'And you think the Swedish airforce is just going to stooge around and watch us while we land and set up camp . . .'

'You won't even see them. Your flight will replace a scheduled civvy run. When you approach your DZ your pilot will report engine trouble to Swedish air traffic control and act like he's got problems. He'll lose altitude and drop you off just before the difficulty miraculously rights itself and he turns away for home. Far as the Swedes are concerned, it'll be a routine flight that just got hairy for a moment or two.'

Ol' Foul Mouth had a way of presenting a mission that Revell didn't like. What had doubtless been long thought over and meticulously worked on by experienced planning Staffs, he made sound hasty and improvised. While riding shotgun for a bunch of gunners wasn't the best job Revell had been offered, it would do as a stopgap, serve to keep the nucleus of his new command together, if it ever materialised. His life seemed a succession of stopgaps; his battles, his women, each briefly enjoyed then discarded as he hurried to the next, and hopefully better experience.

'You'll pick up your equipment and the group you're to escort at Bremen. You'll fly out from there.' Lippincott rose to conclude the meeting. 'Best round up that cut-throat mob of yours, fast as you can. Where are they now, what they doing?'

'Manning a Zone perimeter checkpoint. They'll have their hands too full of refugees to get into any trouble there.'

'You're forgetting I know that crowd, and so do you. Neither of us believe that, not for a fucking second.'

16

TWO

'I hope the lieutenant knows what he's doing. We're supposed to be making sure the refugees stay in the Zone, not helping them get out.' Burke looked out from the uncurtained window, along the road to the checkpoint.

A bedraggled group of elderly civilians was shuffling through the gap that had been opened in the barricade. The moment the last one was clear Lieutenant Hogg hauled the wire-festooned pole back into place, laying it across the top of the concrete-filled oil drums. He was hampered by several of the party attempting to crowd about him and offer their thanks. An old lady in a mud-spattered suede coat kept grabbing at his hand, trying to kiss it.

'Now how far are they going to get, dressed like a load of scarecrows?' Ripper's southern drawl was accentuated by a succession of yawns, and he tucked a blanket more snugly about his legs as he lay slumped on the couch. 'Folks in these parts are shit scared of the Zone, reckon anyone who gets out carries every disease from anthrax to the black death, and glows in the dark to boot. They'll be lucky to travel another mile, and luckier still if all that happens is that they're picked up and shoved back in.'

Ushering the civilians away with a pantomime of urgency, the young officer freed his sleeve from a rusty barb and walked back to the Iron Cow. The hover-APC was parked at the side of the road, straddling the fence it had crushed when it came to rest. Its turret-mounted

Rarden cannon, supposed to be covering the road-block, drooped, and still had its bell-shaped muzzle draped with a scrap of oily cloth against the flurries of sleet.

'He's not doing them any favours. Those Krauts think he's smiling because he's glad to be helping them. If only they knew, he's doing it because he reckons the fighting in the Zone will be simpler if he empties it of civvies.' Burke watched Libby stand aside on the vehicle's lowered front ramp to let the lieutenant in, then once more fill the doorway as he scrutinised the face of each refugee filing past. Totally absorbed in the inspection he was making, he appeared oblivious of the cold and discomfort.

Burke went back to the fire, and tossed on to it a couple of chair legs picked from among the pile of broken furniture that provided its crackling fuel. Their impact sent a mass of sparks up the chimney. 'This isn't a bad little number we've got here. I hope the lieutenant isn't about to louse it up. There's bloody millions of civvies trapped in the Zone. If word gets round that we're holding the door open, the trickle we're getting through this back road at the moment will turn into a ruddy flood. Then there'll be some questions.'

'Hell, what's the worst they can do to us?' Ripper stretched. 'They can only send us back into combat. And they'll be doing that soon enough anyway.'

Using his boot, Burke tried to return an ember to the grate, but only managed to bring down two more. 'I'd prefer it later than sooner. So would Dooley, he can't get visits from his girlfriends in the Zone.'

'Friends they may be, girls never. Leastways, not for a long, long time.' York came out of the kitchen, surrounded by blue smoke. 'The meal might be a little late. The gas must have been cut, there's hardly any pressure.'

'Doesn't seem to be affecting your cooking. You're still burning everything.'

'I'm a fucking good cook, could have been a chef.' He offered Burke the dripping spatula he carried like a badge of office. It wasn't accepted. 'So shut up then.' He listened. A steady 'thump-thump, thump-thump' could be heard. It came from the next room, sounding like heavy furniture being rhythmically bumped into the wall, it went on and on. 'He's never still at it, is he? What can the fucking over-sexed bugger be doing now.'

'I'd say you hit it on the head first time.' Ripper punched the cushions into a more comfortable configuration. 'I reckon he's about done with fucking, and he's started buggering. He sure does like variety. Ain't ever known anybody who liked doing it so many different ways, 'cepting a cousin of mine who kinda got a hankering for the livestock.'

Having failed to return the brand, Burke lost patience with it and crushed it into charcoal dust. 'I don't know about that, but did you see the old piece he took in there?' He nodded at the bedroom door. 'She must be into her fifties, must be.'

'Can't say I've ever been with one that old myself.' Reaching out, Ripper lifted a slim-necked green wine bottle from the side of the fire. He jiggled it against the light to gauge its contents, then pulled the protruding cork with his teeth before taking a long pull at a lukewarm liquid. 'Ain't a touch on a decent rye, but,' screwing up his eyes he examined the label and tried to decipher the elaborate entwined script, 'but I just might be getting a taste for this here schnapps. We stay here much longer and I'll have to see if I can't lay in a supply. Where was I? Oh yeah, like I was saying, I ain't never had one that old. Come to that, apart from a hairy old dame I ran errands for when I was a kid, who used to take out my cock and squeeze it when I got the change wrong, I ain't had no relations with any female over eighteen or so. What do you think they're like when they're getting on a spell, all kinda discoloured and crinkled at the edges, and maybe smelling a bit?'

'Sounds like a description of York's cooking.' The spatula hit the side of the fireplace as Burke ducked.

Only for a moment did the slamming of the kitchen door drown out the continual reverberations of Dooley's excesses in the next room.

A draught of cold air blasted in with Andrea and circled the stuffy room for several seconds after she closed the door behind her She propped her grenade-discharger fitted M16 against the back of the couch before taking off her helmet and slipping out of the glistening rain cape. Draping the dripping garment over the back of the remaining empty chair, she dried her face and hands on the crumpled curtain she took from the top of a sideboard. The large brass rings still attached to it clinked as she rubbed the last beads of icy water from her fringe.

'We will be moving out shortly. The lieutenant said we are to be ready.' There was no need for her to do anything to get the men's attention, she knew before she looked up that she would have an audience.

The surge of cold air and the opening and closing of the doors had woken Clarence; now his head appeared out the top of the sleeping bag against the far wall. 'That will please York. His culinary efforts must be about nearing fruition, or is that a dead goat I can smell?'

'Sod York.' Burke dismissed their volunteer cook's feelings with an airy wave of his hand, then gestured dramatically at the bedroom door, 'Who's going to break Dooley's concentration and give him the bad news.'

The non-stop thump-thumping had become a rapid thumpity-thumping. Andrea heard, understood, and without hesitation crossed the room and grasped the door handle. Ripper jumped from the couch and caught up in time to grab her wrist.

'I don't think that's such a good idea. Either he's going to shoot your pretty head off, or he's gonna reckon you're offering to make up a threesome and then he's liable to grab you before you get a chance to explain.'

'I know his temper, with that I can cope, as for the other . . . I do not think he is suicidal.' Shaking off the restraining grip with ease Andrea pushed into the room.

'Fuck off, I'm busy.' Dooley didn't even slow down, let alone falter. He had the woman bent over a dressing-table against the partition wall, and was frantically taking her from behind, his pants rucked in grubby folds around his ankles.

The ample flesh of the overweight bodies slapped together with a loud wet clapping noise that failed to smother the woman's screams when she realised they were no longer alone.

'We are to be ready to move at once, the major will be back soon.' Andrea's expression didn't alter as she unblinkingly took in the scene.

'I said get out. I don't care if the shitty Russians are coming, I'm coming first.' It was taking all of Dooley's considerable strength to hold the loudly protesting woman, for having failed to break free she now attacked him with her elbows, pounding them back with pile-driver force into his chest and stomach. When she eventually came to the conclusion that her best efforts had failed, she contented herself with sobbing hysterically and hiding her scarlet face in the voluminous lacy French-knickers she had managed to pull down from the corner of the mirror.

'Shit, I can't finish this.' Dooley withdrew, and as he hoisted his pants received a rain of pudgy-fisted blows to the face, as the woman dropped the undergarment and the last vestige of her dignity to launch the assault.

The appearance of York, Burke and Ripper behind Andrea only served to intensify the woman's hysterics. She grabbed her dress from the soiled and rumpled bed and cowered in a corner of the room, shielding herself with one hand, while trying to restore some order to her elaborately-piled hair with the other.

'Don't you ever bloody do that again.' Dooley towered over Andrea. 'I'd have killed one of them grinning monkeys if they'd done it. I was going for a personal best, would have bloody made it too, eventually. Now look what you've done, buggered my screw and reduced a perfectly good piece of knocking fodder to that . . .'

Being pointed at didn't help the woman. She was unsuccessfully trying to conceal her globular white breasts with a fat forearm, while hopping up and down on one leg with a high heel caught in the lace trimming of her knickers. She was sobbing, between alternate distraught snatches of threats and imprecations.

'What's she saying? She's gabbing too fast for me.'

Shrugging, Andrea turned to go out, but answered when Dooley grabbed her arm and spun her about, repeating the question. 'She said she is going to report you. She will tell the police you raped her.'

'Silly cow, she's just worked up, that's all. Her husband's got his own factory, he's in local politics I think, she ain't going to risk queering that, not the nice little life she's got. You speak the lingo better than me, tell her if she does that I'd have to show the cops some of the Polaroids she took of me, at her house. Remind her about the lampshade and the carrot, she'll know what I mean. Well, tell her then, you got me into this fucking mess.'

It was necessary for Andrea to walk right up to the fat frau and slap her face before she was able to get the woman's full attention. As she finished translating Dooley's message the woman stopped her howling, nodded dumbly and muttered a reply, accompanying it with a pleading look at Dooley.

'There will be no accusation of rape, she wishes to forget what has happened.' With that brief translation Andrea went back to the lounge, and the others, unwilling to remain without the presence of her moderating influence, followed.

'And fucking stay out.' Savagely, Dooley kicked the door shut. Shit, why'd they have to burst in then; another minute, well maybe two, and he'd have done it. Hell, he couldn't leave it like this, he had to finish, had to have one last one. If they were moving out it could be ages before he got another chance, and if the major were taking them into action, and that was near enough the only place he ever did take them, then maybe it'd be his last ever. What did he have to lose?

His first attempt to approach the woman met with a violent and shrill rebuff, but he persisted. In halting terrible German he tried to make amends. Within a minute he caught her eye and got a thin embarrassed smile from her. A few more soft words and he was allowed to gently parry the half-hearted pushes with which she attempted to fend him off, while at the same time fastening the front of her wrap-over dress. At his third try Dooley arrested her efforts and slid a large hand between the silky folds to cup a heavy breast. A single muted mew of protest and another even weaker attempt to ward him off were easily overcome.

Dooley ignored the clattering from the next room. Just one more, that was all he wanted, just one more with this juicy great beauty. Come on you big, pink, fat-rumped cock-teaser, quit buggering me about. Now his fingers probed further and played with a warm and rapidly hardening nipple. She was weakening. Hell, he was having to go too fast, at this rate he'd finish screwing up everything but the woman.

Persuading her to sit on the bed beside him, his hand moved from breast to dimpled knee to the soft inside of her ample thighs. A last moment of resistance, and then his hand closed on her silk-shielded underneath. He'd got her, he'd got her. Oh shit, she wanted to waste time with a kiss, alright, just the one, to keep her sweet . . . a sloppy one, but she didn't seem to mind, had even used her tongue for the first time . . . maybe an audience had turned her on.

Should he go for it straight, or risk turning her . . . what the hell, go for broke, neck or nothing . . . or maybe that should be arse or nothing. A fleeting sulky expression as he extracted his exploring fingers from her underwear was swiftly replaced by a slyly conspiratorial mock coyness as he grasped her by the shoulders and began to ease her around.

It was working, it was working! OK, so it wouldn't be an ideal position but he was in too much of a hurry to be fussy. As her knees slid off the bed and she knelt on the floor bent over it, Dooley got down behind her. Shit, it was a hell of a shame having to make it a quicky, but the way he felt it shouldn't be too difficult. Releasing himself from his pants, he held the huge rod of his erection to aim it at the dark tuft of hair showing between the parted thighs. Oh boy, as he enjoyed the moment of penetration he knew it wasn't going to be difficult at all, not at all.

Clarence watched from the window as the Black Hawk transport helicopter made a smooth touchdown in the field across the road from the hotel. Its wheels sank to their hubs in the soft ground as the engine howl died away, and the rotors appeared as individuals from the blurred disc of movement and sent the last stinging shower of spray at the front of the building and towards the road-block and the armoured flank of the Iron Cow. 'The major is here.'

'Well I didn't think it was the fucking tooth fairy making a racket like that.' With more haste than precision Dooley was stuffing his worldly possessions into a couple of scruffy kitbags. 'You knew I was busy, couldn't one of you have done this for me?'

'If your birds weren't so old,' through the partially open bedroom door Burke could see the woman's profile, admired the jut of her mature figure, 'I might have done something on a tit for tat basis, but as I don't fancy wrinkled tit, and you're doing a tatty enough job of packing . . .'

'Piss off.' Cramming in the last few items, Dooley hoisted the lumpy loads to his shoulders. 'Well, I've got everything I want, are we ready?'

'And what about this fucking meal?' Tearing off his gingham apron, York hurled it into the fireplace. Steam and smoke from the kitchen blended and wreathed him.

'It's a meal?' There was a note of incredulity in Ripper's voice. 'Jesus, I didn't know it was a food you were a-cooking, I thought you were working on a new poison gas.' He craned to look past the cook at the heaving brown sludge filling a pan on the stove, 'or maybe a new substitute for bitumen . . .'

A dagger-laced glare and a snort of contempt was York's only comment. He grabbed hold of the pan, momentarily looking as if he was about to throw it, then he went to the fire and poured the entire contents over the flames. At least he turned the pan over, but the contents proved reluctant to abandon it and clung tight, until several increasingly vigorous shakes dislodged a solid lump. The fire died instantly.

'And that is probably the effect it would have had on us.' Double-checking the fastenings on his sniper rifle's waterproof cover, Clarence led them from the room, down, and out of the building.

'Get aboard the chopper, we're leaving the hover-APC here.' Revell threw them the news while they were still complaining about the cold. Folding his arms and adopting a belligerent air, Burke stood his ground as the others filed towards the aircraft. 'I've been nursing that bastard machine for six months, just got the git working how I like it, and now you bloody tell me I've got to leave it here, to be stripped by sodding looters or wrecked by some idiot driver who doesn't know how to handle her. Major, you know how scarce these wagons are, how the hell will we ever lay our hands on another?'

'You finished?'

Burke opened his mouth to go on, but realised the officer wasn't offering him an invitation to continue, and closed it again.

'Now, unless you want to be pulling every stinking back-breaking job around for the next thirty days, I suggest you shut up and listen.' Revell had been expecting an outburst from the British combat driver, but couldn't let him get away with it, hence the threat. It was a particularly effective one in Burke's case. Except where his beloved hover-APC was concerned – and even then he'd take every opportunity to hive a task off on to someone else – he was the most dedicated, the most skilful exponent of the art of goldbricking in the whole of NATO. 'You know damned well that old bus is way overdue for a complete refit The powered traverse it out, the electrics are still held together by prayers and Blu-tack after that last brush we had with the Commies and the port turbine is developing a mind all of its own. There's a recovery crew on its way, but if you want to say a last goodbye to the ugly great hunk of metal you can go tell the lieutenant I'll see him and the rest of the squad at the chopper the moment our West German reliefs arrive.'

As he watched Burke trudging towards the roadblock,

head down against the gusting wind, Revell noticed a movement at an upper window of the hotel. There weren't supposed to be any civvies still around . . . He turned to look at the chopper in time to see Dooley waving back from the cabin doorway. The big man vanished inside the moment he realised he'd been observed. So Burke wasn't the only one who was pushing his luck today. Oh, what the hell, let him get away with it this once, pretend he hadn't noticed, the big gorilla had been behaving himself for the best part of a week. Anyway, it was most likely Hogg's fault. Doubtless the lieutenant had been eating and sleeping in the Iron Cow, and had kept Sergeant Hyde too busy with a thousand niggling tasks for him to keep tabs on the big man every minute of the day – and it only ever took a minute for Dooley to get organised. Presented with a building chock-full of bedrooms it was obvious what he'd been up to . . .

'Where are we going?' Libby stood with Burke and the lieutenant outside the vehicle, as Sergeant Hyde made a final check of all the lockers and hatches. They could hear the sharpened studs of his boots grating on the hull's metal floor.

'No bloody idea.' Burke thrust his hands deep into his pockets. 'But I hope it's somewhere a fuck sight warmer than this.'

'I'm not leaving the Zone.'

'You've got no sodding choice, mate,' Burke tried stamping to aid his circulation. 'Where that whirly-bird goes, there go we, like it or not. You're not planning to do something stupid, are you?'

It was beginning to get dark, there would be no more refugees now, Libby knew that – they only travelled during daylight so as to stand the best chance of spotting mines – but he kept looking up the road, willing just one more to appear, a slim attractive girl. There was no one. No Helga. He'd stopped showing the photo to the passing human debris: not one of them had eyes for it, they were too full of themselves, too wrapped up in the overwhelming emotions of relief, joy and even disbelief at having finally made it. He had to get back into the Zone again, had to.

'Well, are you?'

'Mind your own business.'

Taking a tight hold on Libby's sleeve, Burke pulled him away from the group. 'It *is* my sodding business. If the brass have laid on a chopper for us that means we're going places in a hurry, and that means Ol' Foul Mouth has found another bastard job for us. I don't fancy going into action with some last minute replacement beside me, some ruddy unknown who might put me right in it.'

'It's nice to know I'd be missed.' There was a sneer in the words.

Sergeant Hyde came out on to the ramp, jumped down, and activated the door control. He had to hit the switch twice before the hydraulics eventually, reluctantly, raised and closed it. 'All secure, Lieutenant. Be a good idea if we boarded the chopper now.' The lipless, graft-patched edges of his mouth hardly moved as he spoke.

'The major said to hang on until our reliefs arrived.'

'So I heard, Lieutenant, but I can see a Bundeswehr truck coming. The bunch of refugees in the back look familiar, and that's a military police jeep following it.'

'Yes, well maybe we could board now.' Shepherding the men before him, Hogg kept glancing back at the approaching vehicles.

Hyde was the last to scramble in, and did so as the officers went forward and the Black Hawk lifted. Before closing the sliding door he saw the jeep stop at the road-block and its occupants climb out to watch the take-off. They didn't look too happy.

The men were already making themselves comfortable, which in most cases meant settling down to sleep. Andrea sat next to Dooley, who held his mirror-polished bayonet and was stabbing and cutting the air as he spoke to illustrate his words.

Through a misted window, Hyde caught a last glimpse

27

of the hotel. There would have been big trouble if they'd stayed, but then, as yet, they didn't know what sort of trouble the major was taking them into. Chances were it would be a hundred times worse, a thousand times more deadly. Maybe down there was a frying pan they'd soon be happy to leap back into, those of them still able to leap.

THREE

Sergeant Hyde stood at the foot of the steps and scanned the distant gate in the perimeter fence as the first of the Starlifter's engines burst into life. He checked his watch for the tenth time in a minute and pretended not to see the flight crew urgently beckoning him to board from the cockpit window. They were cutting it fine. The timing had to be precise if they were to slot into the air traffic pattern in place of the scheduled civilian flight without attracting attention.

He was aware of Revell standing in the doorway at the top of the steps and knew that he too would be counting off each second until the moment when they would be able to delay no longer.

There was a freezing wind whistling across the open ground at the end of the taxiway, but Hyde made no concession to it by pushing his hands into his pockets or pulling up the hood of his parka. He liked the cold, and besides, he hardly felt it on his face as it struck at the deadened nerves in the rebuilt tissue.

'Can't leave it much longer, Sergeant . . .'

He heard the major's shout at the same moment as he spotted the jeep that was racing and bucking across the grass towards them in defiance of every airport regulation. As the distance narrowed he made out Burke behind the wheel, and a sullen-faced Libby sat in the back, flanked by Clarence and Dooley.

The ground crew were finishing their work and boarding their transport as the jeep rocked to a stop, cutting four brown gashes in the soaked and ice particle-laden grass at the edge of the concrete.

Even as Hyde followed the others up into the aircraft, the steps were being hitched for towing, and he had to jump a widening gap to board.

'I always say, if you got to go to war, then if you can't do it in style at least do it comfort.' Ripper slumped in the seat and put his feet up on the back of the row in front.

'You've got a funny idea of being comfortable.' A dozen cigarette stubs and matches were strewn about Burke's feet on the floor of the sled-mounted cabin. An echo of the vibration from the aircraft's hull kept them in slight but perceptible motion. 'Mind you, one of these would make a nice bingo hall.' He surveyed the serried rows of safety harness equipped seats. 'You could even strap the old girls down, make sure they stayed for an extra card and stop them collecting their winnings.'

'Where's everyone else?' Arching his back to relieve the aches caused by an abortive attempt to sleep stretched out along a row, York peered around.

'The artillery lads are scrambling about on the two sleds at the back. They've got a real eager beaver of a captain and a sergeant-major who looks like he eats privates for breakfast.' Yet another spent match was flicked away as Burke finished the second packet of the day, and sent it, crumpled, in its wake. 'The others are in the crew room behind the flight-deck, they've got coffee there.'

'So long as the sergeant-major only eats his own privates, or beavers, I ain't bothered, and I'll wait for the crowd to clear around the coffee.' York dipped his hand into Ripper's bag of large white mints and helped himself. The moment he tasted the first one, he put the others back. 'This is a heck of a long hop. I thought we were going into action on the west coast of Sweden, not the other side of Mongolia.'

'The major says we're taking a scenic route, just to

make sure we get thoroughly lost among the civvy traffic.' With three vigorous puffs Burke reduced the king-sized cigarette's length by half, bringing its glowing tip that much nearer his heavily nicotine-stained fingers. 'We're just as bloody likely to get shot down tiddling about like this as we would be if we hedge-hopped straight there. Apart from the chances of the Swedes or the Ruskies noticing we're not what we're supposed to be, we're bloody likely to get shopped by any civvy pilot who gets a whiff of what's going on. They don't take too kindly to having their lives made more dangerous by the military using the civvy routes as cover.'

'Now why don't you relax.' Giving every appearance of intending to follow his own advice, Ripper slumped lower in his seat, so that his oversized helmet was tipped forward by the back of the chair, over his eyes. 'This is like travelling first-class, compared to what it was like in that SAC Galaxy I came over in. Why hell, if we asked real nice maybe the lovely little Andrea would do the stewardess bit. She could give me in-flight or indecent attention anytime.'

'Where is she anyway?' Standing on a seat, York looked over the rows. 'She don't seem the sort to go and have a chat and a coffee.'

'I should imagine she's head of the queue to ask the major for permission to bump off our pet Commie.' A new packet was extracted from a deep pocket and Burke lit his forty-first cigarette.

'I bet that guy Clarence is crowding close behind her. Why've we got our own tame Ruskie anyway?' Ripper was indignant. 'What can he do we can't?'

Burke watched ash float slowly to the floor now greying about his feet. 'Talk fluent Russian for a start. What do you think we got all that extra radio gear for? When things get hot the Commies won't have time for piddling about with coding. If we can monitor what they're jabbering about it could be bloody useful, especially if they're nattering about how much shit they'll be shovelling in our direction.' The smirk that Burke turned on was aimed at York. 'He'll be keeping you busy.'

'I'll have enough to do, keeping the command links open in the face of the jamming the Reds are bound to try, without having to help out a cruddy amateur. The way I see it, chances are I'll end up working all the equipment and that beetle-browed shitty sod will be operating nothing more difficult than his notepad and pencil.'

'Well, ain't we just lucky to have such a brilliant radio operator. You reckon you'll be able to cope alright then?'

The gentle sarcasm was lost on York, and he took no exception to Ripper's remark. 'Of course I will, but that's not the damned point, I shouldn't have to. For this job I ought to be a corporal at least, with a couple of guys under me.' He suddenly noticed the looks the others were exchanging. 'You know what I mean.'

'Course we do.' Only the top of Ripper's helmet was now visible, and his voice floated out from between the rows. 'You want a couple of guys under you, that's fine, so long as you don't want me for one. I prefer girls. There ain't ever been no faggots in my family, we've all been dead straight, 'cepting that fifth cousin I heard tell of, the one who got kinda fond of livestock, if you get my drift.'

Several of the filter tips began to roll sluggishly in the ash as the aircraft banked to a fresh heading. Pulling out his small compass, Burke checked the new direction. It was south-east. They were beginning the final run. Removing another cigarette from the pack before he had finished the last he took another long look around the cabin. Well it seemed strong enough, and he'd examined the great steel skids below it earlier, but every time he thought of the way they were leaving the aircraft his stomach fluttered and he broke out in a sweat. If there had been even a pretence of a steering mechanism to hold on to, it would have helped.

When those huge chutes popped and dragged the cabin-sled out, every one of them, strapped helpless in their seats, was going to be at the mercy of blind luck.

The aircraft struck turbulence and dipped before recovering. For a terrifying moment Burke had wildly imagined that the drop was coming now, that there had been an accident and he and the cabin were about to start a long and steepening dive into the freezing water of the Kattegat. His hand shook as he lit another cigarette.

'What you got there?' Sergeant Hyde leant over Clarence's shoulder and tried to see what he had so hurriedly stuffed into his pack. He reached in and pulled out the surprisingly heavy small screw-top cannister. Barely the size of a modest Thermos flask, it felt like it weighed twenty pounds or more.

'You quite sure you want to undo it, Sarge?'

There was nothing in the sniper's tone that conveyed threat or warning, but Hyde hesitated before taking hold of the top and starting to unscrew it.

'Don't.'

Hyde turned to see that it was Libby who had grabbed his wrist. 'I've just about had enough of you. The major may have laid on that last minute trip to the refugee registry for you, but you're not under any special protection. I'm warning you . . .'

'Go ahead then, but I'm warning *you*, Sarge. You undo that and you might lose your nuts as well as your face, or at least the use of them.' Not for a moment did Libby relax his hold, until Hyde slackened his grip on the container top, then he let go fast and took a step back.

'What's in this?' Although he repeated the question, there was a hardening suspicion in the NCO's mind.

'I think you know what's in it, Sarge, but if you want to make sure then go ahead, open it by all means. Be my guest.' Taking a sip at his coffee and pulling a face at the taste, Clarence reached out for and took the weighty cylinder from Hyde's grasp.

'How many rounds have you got?' Libby maintained his distance.

'Six.'

The crowd that had gathered drew back as the sniper undid the top and pulled out a single 7.62mm NATO rifle round, unremarkable except for its exceptional length and

3

the unusual yellow and purple colour code bands about its tip.

'Really, there's nothing to be afraid of. The depleted uranium core is in a lead sheath.'

'I'm the armourer, remember.' Along with all of the others, Libby was staying well clear. 'Those little buggers were withdrawn a year ago. The shielding's inadequate. What the hell do you want with them?'

Clarence casually rolled the bullet in his palm, making no move to replace it. 'On two recent occasions I've been in good positions for clear shots at Commie officers; long-range, but nothing exceptional. I've hit them and seen them go down, only to watch them get to their feet a few minutes later and sprint for cover under their own power. One of them offered himself a second time, and I only put him down permanently by using a head shot. They're wearing a new type of body armour, it can't be anything else . . .'

'I ain't heard nothing about no new body armour.'

Clarence brushed Dooley's interruption aside. 'Neither have I, but I've seen the evidence. I'm telling you, at a hundred yards or more, the worst those Ruskie officers suffered was a temporary loss of wind and dignity. I want to kill them, not play pat-a-cake. When they go down I want them to stay there, like they usually do.'

There was movement among the front rank of men gathered about the sniper, and Andrea pushed through. She lifted the bullet from his hand and examined it. 'I thought that these were to be used against light armoured vehicles, or gunners behind shields.'

Retrieving the bullet, Clarence put it back in the cylinder. 'That was their original use, yes, but if they'll punch through sixty millimetres of plate at two hundred yards they'll certainly go through this new personal protection the Ruskies are bringing into use, maybe out to six hundred yards or better.'

'If those fancy flak-jackets have got a metal insert, you'll get the added bonus that they'll burst into flame, whoosh.' Dooley turned the flame of his lighter to maximum and watched the six-inch pillar of flickering yellow.

'So long as the core goes on to do its job, I don't care if it paints them red, white and blue on impact.' To end the exchange, Clarence stuffed the container into his pack and concentrated on his coffee. It was all a lot of fuss over nothing, like the mystique that surrounded the atomic demolition troops. Those men thought nothing of racing about the countryside in jeeps, toting suitcase-sized nukes; well, he felt the same about the bullets filled with spent fissionable material. He'd used them when they were first issued, though the strict guidelines had imposed severe limitations on their application on the battlefield. That and the fact that situations where they were suitable or available were not all that common. Even then, by the time he'd observed all the governing regulations, and perhaps first had to eject an already chambered standard cartridge, the moment when he could have used one had often passed.

Now though, he was glad he'd hung on to the bullets, even though coming up with a plausible excuse for not handing them in had not been easy at the time. There was no way he was going to stand by and watch the artillery lads enjoy all of the action. He would find a way to have some portion of it for himself, as large a slice as he could possibly carve.

'I suppose it could be worse, but I don't see how.' The pilot handed the weather report to Major Revell. 'That's ten-tenths cloud, heavy snow, and winds gusting at twenty plus from the south and south-west. Forecast says the wind will drop, but not soon enough to do us any good.'

Revell barely glanced at the page torn from the message pad. He'd hardly needed the pilot's summary either. By following the frequent updates for the DZ he'd gained a good idea of the steadily deteriorating general weather conditions. 'This mission is important, can you still drop us?'

'According to the orders I've got, I drop you, period. I presume that means regardless of weather or anything else from acts of God down. Either this mission is as important as you say, Major, or you got big enemies back at Headquarters.'

The Starlifter pitched in fierce turbulence, the autopilot correcting the violent motion before the pilot could over-ride it. 'Will you look at that. I don't ever get the chance to do any real flying ... Like I say though, someone must really have it in for you. Have you crossed anyone real important lately, a three-star general, or maybe a HQ clerk? Tell you what, I wish I weren't included in the risk with you. I've got eight flight-deck and handling crew who feel the same.'

'How big is the risk under these conditions?' It was Lieutenant Hogg who asked. He'd seen that their Russian was settled on a spare fold-down seat alongside the flight engineer's control console, and now took an interest, a very personal interest, in the conversation.

'Look, I'm no scaremonger, maybe it's better you don't know. This is a case where ignorance could be real bliss. What you don't know you can't worry over, and anyway, I'm the pilot, I'm the one who has to place the drop . . .'

'And we're the ones who have to make it, so tell us.'

The pilot's hands rested lightly on the control column, riding with the movements dictated by the autopilot to whose cut-off his eyes kept straying. 'OK, first, low altitude parachute extraction is strictly a clear skies assignment. If we have this,' he indicated the large flakes of snow self-destructing against the windows in rapid succession, 'then we also have problems. We've got all sorts of fancy gizmos on board, they'll give me precise altitude so I let you go at the right height, and position so I let you go in the right place; what I haven't got is a gadget that, as we go barrelling in at zero feet plus a bit in white-out conditions, is going to tell me whether or not there's a clump of trees or a building dead ahead.' Again his hand flirted with the autopilot cut-off, but withdrew. 'Those sleds you're going down on travel quite a ways after they touch. There's three in the drop, so allowing for intervals between each, on an island two miles long I have to find a half mile stretch of reasonably flat land, blindfolded.'

'Is there anything else, or is that the extent of the horror story?' Hogg heard the pilot, but kept his eyes on the Russian. The man sat impassively, his heavy-jowelled face revealing no hint of emotion or reaction to the words he must have understood.

'You want more?' The pilot turned round in his seat. 'Alright then, try this on. These big babies were never meant for this work. Starlifters were designed as strategic transports, heavy load, long haul, that's their business. OK, so this is one of the early models and it's been modified and re-allocated to tactical re-supply work, but it still isn't happy hedge-hopping about the place, piddling about with nickel and dime loads that a prop-job could handle.'

'Just so long as you put us down on the right island, that's all we ask.' Revell cut into the exchange.

'That we can promise, we're just not offering any guarantees as to what sort of condition your men and equipment will be in by the time the sleds come to a stop.'

Ignoring the pilot's chuckle, Revell found his own eyes straying to the Russian. It was the first time he'd worked with one of the many deserters from the Warsaw Pact armies. The man was an archetypical Russian; stocky build, dark deep-set eyes, with heavy features that betrayed little of his thoughts and no hint of any capacity for humour. Perhaps it was because of his appearance, and the fact that his actual name, Vasili Shalamov, did not trip readily from the tongue, that everyone had taken to calling him Boris. He wondered what the man's reasons were not just for deserting – God knows there were enough reasons for men to leave the Soviet forces by any means they could – but for volunteering his services to NATO. The lengthy screening process he'd have been subjected to should have weeded him out if he was a plant, but some always got through and had built a mountain of distrust towards their sort as a whole. Only rarely were they assigned any task other than rear-area or pioneer work, and then only under the very strictest supervision, though with the growing numbers involved, there were rumours of the formation of Free-Russian combat units.

'Is the island inhabited?'

The accent was impeccable textbook English that would not have been out of place on a BBC news bulletin. Revell hadn't been told what rank the Russian had held; but he must have at the very least been the equivalent of a technical sergeant, first-grade. His immediate reaction to the question was to ignore it. The instinct sprang in part from his natural distaste for contact of any sort with a people that two years of barbaric warfare had taught him to hate, and partly from a distrust that all the assurances from I-Corp could not shake off. But damn it, the man was going with them, was taking the same risks, more if he came to be captured, and in any event he'd soon learn the truth for himself.

'No, not now. Before the war the west coast of Sweden was a popular tourist area in summer. There's a few holiday homes on the island, mostly the converted houses of what used to be a small fishing community, and the remains of an old castle at the northern tip. The rest of it is much the same as the hundreds of other islands along the coast.'

'You still have much to learn about the Russian mind.' Boris watched the fuel gauges on the engineer's panel ticking away the fractions of tons of fuel with each mile they travelled. 'In the West to be among a crowd is to be safe; in Russia, to be among a crowd is to invite danger.'

'Either way, you're about to find out.' The pilot eased his headphones off and called back to Revell. 'I've got Malmo tower on; in five minutes I start my lame duck routine. You better board your bus.'

For the fifth time Burke checked his seatbelt, tightening it yet again. He'd positioned himself in the second row, so

38

that by holding on to the back of the seat in front he at least had the illusion of a degree of control over what was about to happen. The flashing red light high up on the front bulkhead gave off a continuous glow. Two more minutes. At one and the same time he wanted to get it over with, and for it never to happen. It seemed as if his heartbeat was counting down the seconds to the moment when the rams would push the sled back along the fuselage, the chutes would deploy and they'd be snatched out into space. Closing his eyes to hide the still unlit green bulb from his sight didn't help, it only made the clock inside him louder, until its pumping roar filled his ears.

Revell was the last to take his place. As he sat down alongside Hyde in the back row he took a final look across the several rows of seats. The two groups had remained clannishly separate, with most of the artillery men occupying the left of the cabin. It made him think of a neatly packed box of toy soldiers, waiting for the next game. An involuntary shudder ran through him as he fastened his lap and shoulder straps together. Had Hyde noticed it? He gave no sign, but then none was ever to be found in the British sergeant's face.

Now the aircraft was pitching more violently and the movement was being transmitted to the men, even through the sprung floor of the cabin. To Revell it was a sure sign that they were right down low, making the final approach.

The green light went on, its brightness blotting out the red even as it faded, then that too was extinguished as a sudden jarring lurch severed the cabin's umbilical link with the aircraft's systems with a jerk.

They were on their way.

FOUR

The cabin moved more smoothly as the powerful rams overcame the initial resistance of the metal runners. Dooley felt the aircraft rise as the first sled went out, noting the pilot's immediate correction to the controls. He sensed they were moving faster, then the Starlifter soared again as the second sled followed. It was their turn next. He clamped his teeth on the piece of rubber he'd been given and closed his eyes against the sensation he knew was coming.

There was a savage wrenching acceleration and suddenly the cabin seesawed wildly and the contents of his stomach raced for his throat. His mouth filled with foul taste and he was conscious of being weightless one moment and undergoing the stress of several 'g' the next, as the brake parachutes levelled the yawing sledge and violently checked its speed.

Dooley only had an instant to register the total silence and absence of vibration as he opened his eyes to the pitch-black of the interior, then the runners made their first contact with the ground. Despite all the springing, it felt as though a thousand sets of steel-shod boots were trying to kick his backside over the moon. That was followed immediately by a second massive jolt, and then the world burst apart.

A torrent of bricks and splintered beams, lit by sheets of sparks, hurtled in through the crushed left front of the cabin. Glass and fragments of wood scythed from the dust

41

and crashed into the walls of the cabin, some of them clattering and rebounding from the steel helmets of the men crouched low in their seats.

'Stay where you are. Stay in your seats.' Even as Hyde's bellow filled the interior, the thunder of the collision ceased abruptly and his shouted words encountered no competition for the men's attention.

Canted over at a steep angle, the first frantic attempts at movement by some of the men had caused the cabin to rock and threaten to turn over. The pitching ceased as they resumed their places.

It was quiet, except for a low moaning coming from the front. A torch flicked on, its beam picking out the dust filling the air as its circle of pale yellow illumination lit up the extent of the damage.

Hyde cautiously began to unfasten his harness, then had to grab at the loose ends to stop himself being thrown to the floor as the cabin lurched sideways and slid downhill to a second, more gentle collision than the first. Blasts of ice-cold air whirled snow into the cabin through the gaps among the debris wedged into the damaged front quarter.

Though resting at a steep angle, the cabin seemed more firmly settled than before, and as a second torch was brought into action Revell gave the order for the men to release themselves.

Outside there was a strange jostling clinking noise, like broken bottles being rolled together in a blanket. It had a rhythmic quality, regular and even.

'Hey, we're taking in water.' It was York who announced the discovery, as he moved to help a bombardier trying to free a gunner pinned against the wall.

'Keep calm.' The babble of sound that greeted the information signalled a warning to Revell, and he acted fast to prevent a panic. A quick examination showed that the water was not rising. That and the fact that the cabin was not moving suggested that they were firmly beached at the water's edge. 'Sergeant Hyde, take two men and scout our position. Find somewhere for the casualties, preferably with room enough to take the command centre as well.'

Nodding to Clarence and Libby, Hyde left through the small emergency hatch in the roof. As soon as the trio had gone, Revell turned his attention to the chaos of the interior.

There were eight dead, all gunners, including the battery commander and sergeant-major. Both men had been pierced by the same spear-like splintered floorboard. The fifteen injured included Lieutenant Hogg, whose broken nose was pouring blood in a seemingly endless stream, and Boris, who had been hit in the face by flying rubble and was heavily cut and bruised about the mouth and eyes. Most of the other injuries were multiple fractures of the chest and limbs.

'Come on, Burke, you can let go now.' York was having to prise the driver's fingers from the back of the seat in front. As fast as he or Andrea levered one digit free, another would snap back to re-establish the vice-like grip. We've landed. You're not fucking hurt, give us a hand.'

It quickly became apparent that the front doors were too badly crushed and jammed into their surrounds to be opened without cutting gear. It was just as obvious that getting the injured out through the roof hatches would be virtually impossible.

'I want a hole in that wall, Dooley, get to it.' Panning the torch about, Revell sought someone to wield their other axe. 'You give him a hand, Burke. If you don't like it in here, this is your chance to make your own way out.'

The offer worked where nothing York had said had succeeded. In an instant Burke was up from his seat, had snatched the small bright-bladed axe and was attacking the angle-iron braced alloy wall.

An arm floated in the eighteen inches of water that filled one corner, adding the final touch that made the din-filled cabin into an audio-visual modern version of a surrealist nightmare. The blend of the horrific and the absurd was perfect, and the flickering beams displayed each in turn.

Reversing, the axe, Dooley hammered flat the ragged edges of metal left by Burke's energetic, but more frantic than planned, efforts.

'That'll do. Start moving the casualties. I want to get away from this shoreline as soon as Sergeant Hyde returns.' Revell helped an artillery man with a broken arm to the improvised exit.

'He's here now.' Moving aside to let the NCO back in, Dooley caught and gashed his hand on a ragged protuberance he'd missed. The annoyance he gave vent to in a burst of voluble swearing was directed more at the tear in his glove than at the cut or its cause.

Learning by Dooley's example, Hyde climbed in carefully. 'Our sled came down through the centre of the village. I spotted a house at the far end that's in better condition than most, still got some of its glass. There's a bit of a bank to get the injured up first, then it's near enough level all the way.' The torches caught and made sparkle the particles of ice trapped in the fur edge of Hyde's hood. More flying crystals rode the draught past him.

'Right, post a couple of sentries, everyone else is to give a hand moving the casualties. If a Swedish patrol boat goes past now we'll stand out like a damned neon sign. Soon as that's organised I'll want the other sledges found and their loads transferred to the house or the launch sites. OK, let's move. There's lots to do and not too many of us to do it.'

'What about them?' Andrea indicated the slumped, immobile forms occupying several seats.

Revell knew her well enough to realise she didn't feel the slightest concern for what became of the bodies. She was probing him again, testing him for his reaction, his response to a situation. Just for once he found himself thinking her way. 'Leave them.' It was what he added that marked the difference between them. 'The living come first.'

Standing at the top of the bank down which the cabin had made the final plunge, the bitter wind plucked at them. The snow was beginning to settle, gathering in the ruts gouged out of the grass slope by their descent and softening the harsh outlines of the partially demolished house twenty feet above their heads.

The clattering, clinking noise they'd heard was less noticeable now, as the sea refroze and bound together the shattered slabs of ice.

It had been Libby's idea to use one of the seats from the cabin as an improvised litter on which to hoist their casualties to the top. With three men hauling from above, and two climbing alongside to prevent it tipping, the contraption had made the task of moving the fracture cases to the higher ground easier, and much faster, than it otherwise would have been.

'That was the last of them, Major.' As Libby sought a large block of rubble to which he could secure the rope, a tottering chimney hanging over the ruin finally gave up resistance to the wind's pressure and fell.

Tumbling over the mound of debris, the heavy mass of battered brickwork bounced down the bank, narrowly missing Dooley, who was arranging a corner of the camouflage netting draped over the cabin. It skidded across the ice-crusted gravel at the water's edge and on to the frozen sea, breaking through and disappearing. The fragments of ridge-crossed ice closed over, and the trail of bubbles that rose to the surface was trapped by the lace-like layer that filled the gaps between the pieces.

Revell tugged his hood closer about his face, pulling the fur over his mouth and breathing hard into it so that it warmed his lips. The sensation was quickly lost. He felt the fur harden to frosty spikes the instant it was touched by the wind. That weather forecast, bad as it was, must have been on the optimistic side, it was far colder than he'd expected: far colder even than anything he'd experienced on exercises in the Arctic, and he'd thought them tough at the time.

They'd got off to a bad start. The effective strength of the artillery contingent had already been halved, and their command structure wiped out down to the level of a bombardier. There would be a lot of work for those who were left, and much of the responsibility would fall on the gunner NCO. If he shaped up, it would take some of the load off himself, Hyde and Lieutenant Hogg; but if he didn't, then nursemaiding him would be yet another burden. Even as he speculated the bombardier appeared at Revell's side.

'Casualties have all been transferred, Major. I've got my men sorted and I'd like to get cracking and find our equipment as soon as possible, sir.'

That had been unexpected. The bombardier had slipped on the mantle of command very quickly . . . too quickly? It was tempting to give him his head, but Revell decided that until he knew the youngster's capabilities it would be sensible to restrain, or at least contain, his enthusiasm. 'We'll be doing that in just a minute. What's your speciality?'

'Radar and fire-control systems, sir.'

'OK, pick what men you need, as few as possible, and stick to that. The rest of us will take care of moving and siting the launchers.' For a fraction of a second it seemed that the bombardier might dispute the order, his face had fallen when most of his men had been removed from his command; but he obviously decided against it, executed an impeccable salute and departed.

Checking his watch, Revell noted that they only had nine hours of darkness left. If they couldn't get finished they might have to risk working during the day. Speed was everything now. 'Sergeant Hyde, stop those men clowning about and get them up here, now.'

Hyde had already observed the antics of Dooley and York as they attempted to mount the slippery bank. They were hauling themselves up by the rope, but even so, making hard work of it. His annoyance was increased substantially by the fact that the American officer had noticed and commented on the charade before he'd done so himself.

'Get a bloody move on, Dooley. You're the one who's supposed to be super fit, the muscle man. I've an old grey-haired aunt who could climb that faster.'

46

Reaching the top, Dooley paused before attempting the final heave that would pull him on to level ground. 'I've already been up and down the fucking thing a couple of dozen times, shoving that crappy seat and its passengers. Shit, even I run out of puff sometimes.' The sergeant's boot hovered above his fingers, threatening to crush them into the frozen soil. 'But maybe I can summon up a little extra,' he added as he saw the danger to his precarious handhold.

Still clutching the rope, unable to climb past Dooley's obstructing bulk, York started complaining.

'Shut your racket.' Hyde reached down and jerked the radio-man to his feet as soon as Dooley was out of the way. 'Useless pair of buggers, join the others.'

For a moment York thought he might risk a reply, but Revell was close by, and though he might have chanced it with the British sergeant, there was no way he'd take the same risk with his own officer. Hyde was hard, but Revell was just plain cruel. Even a tough nut like Dooley never tried anything with the major around.

Before he started out for the house, York made a final examination of their handiwork. That was a good job they'd made of camouflaging the sledge and cabin. With the snow beginning to fall heavily, sprinkling the mottled fabric strips sewn to the net, the whole thing was starting to merge with its surroundings. It would already be virtually invisible to the naked eye at more than a few yards.

For the next couple of hours there would be sufficient residual heat from the bodies for the cabin's temperature to remain above that of the terrain surrounding it. Revell knew it wouldn't be much, but it would be enough to stand out on the infra-red screen of any patrolling Swedish or Russian craft doing a sweep of the islands. It was no longer sufficient to hide an object from sight, and camouflage of that sort was not always worth the vast effort frequently involved.

Multi-spectral surveillance made it virtually impossible to keep anything from the prying lens and sensors of the latest photographic and electronic detectors. It was crazy, but maybe the time had come when it would be better to leave important installations such as radar sites and head-quarters out in the open. With an enemy like the Communists, who never took anything at face value and who attributed the same evil cunning to others that they practised themselves, maybe they'd get away with it. It was a tempting idea . . . possibly a bright-eyed young staff officer back at the Pentagon was already pushing such a proposal . . . but as he stood beside York surveying the cabin, he was well aware it was an experiment they dare not try here and now. As it was, in this frozen landscape their every move would stand out like a neon sign. The odds stacked against them were long enough already, there was no reason to help them lengthen.

Eight dead and nearly twice that number injured, with the severity of their wounds varying in degree from Lieutenant Hogg's broken nose to the gunner who'd lost his forearm. Revell knew the calculations as to the minimum numbers of men necessary to carry out the mission had been finely worked out. Now there was a double, a triple workload for those still fit to do it. As he turned into the wind, felt his face smart and his eyes start to water, he could only hope that the worst misfortune likely to befall them before they went into action was now out of the way.

It was their sniper, Clarence, who blamed a malevolent God for everything that went wrong. Not that he had much time for religion himself, but Revell had a feeling that in this war God was neutral, had seen the horrors of the Zone and washed his hands of it. There were many mere mortals inside the Zone who wished they could do the same.

'I've had it. I've fucking had it up to here.' Burke picked up a piece of track plate and shied it at the growing pile of broken weaponry. 'You just wouldn't fucking credit it, would you. I get dropped from the back of a ruddy plane, watch blokes getting smashed to bits all around me. I flog meself to bleeding death carting the poor sods to cover, get dragged out into the wilds of bloody Scandinavia to hunt the sledges before I've even had time for a sodding fag, and now I bloody find the reason I'm bloody here in the first place don't ruddy exist any more.'

'The rocket launchers and the electronics equipment is intact, that is all that is important.' Andrea had hardly paid any attention to the shattered remains of tractor unit. She was sorting through the scattered debris of the sled and its load, joining the others in search of the squad's support weapons and ammunition.

'We're lucky the whole lot didn't just go up on impact.' Dragging aside a twisted girder that had braced the underside of the sledge, Libby scrutinised the battered contents of a crushed ammunition box by torchlight. 'If this stuff alone had gone off,' he removed a mangled anti-tank missile from the tangle of two others, 'the Swedes or their Commie mates would have been down on us like a ton of steaming shit. They'd have had us pinpointed in seconds.'

Burke took in the overturned tractor and the splintered remnants of its packing case load, sticking out from beneath the broken track-festooned wreck. 'Sod it. What am I going to do?' To Burke's mind the sole redeeming feature of a mission concerning which he'd always had the very deepest misgivings had been torn from him. He wasn't about to find consolation in Libby's words.

'How's about you stop blubbering over that old bus that you can't put together again anyhow, and start giving a hand with some of the chores. This stuff gets kinda heavy after the first three.' Staggering under the weight of the cased ammunition already in his arms, Ripper had to accept a fourth heavily-dented box from Hyde before he was allowed to totter off towards the house.

'It's no good, Sarge.' Hardly bothering to glance at it, York tossed a machine gun on to the stack. 'This is just a waste of time. What wasn't mashed on impact got bent when the tractor broke loose and turned over. Look at it.'

He held up one of the decoy mortar-dischargers, all six barrels were now decidedly oval.

'Keep looking. Everything repairable must be salvaged, and everything else must be gathered up into one place, so we can get it ready for effective demolition. We can't go round sticking a couple of ounces of plastic on each individual chunk of rubbish.' Diving on the butt of a machine gun, Hyde dragged it from beneath the crushed tractor cab: but that was all there was, the barrel and body of the weapon had been torn off and pounded into the ground.

'It was the chutes.' Carrying part of the rigging, Revell led Clarence and Dooley into the clearing.

The two men were having difficulty with the huge bundle of canopy silk. It kept trailing and snagging on the ragged stumps of silver birch that had been felled by the sleds' high-speed impact.

'One of the shits didn't deploy properly, must have wrapped itself around the others.' Dumping the voluminous folds of fine fabric on the pile, and weighting them down with anonymous hunks of metal, Dooley pulled a face. 'Good job this set weren't on our rig, we'd have gone straight through that fucking house and on out to sea.'

'We'd have been alright with York around.'

The radio-man treated Libby's comment with suspicion. 'And why's that?'

'With that big mouth of yours, you could have drunk it dry and we'd have been able to walk home.'

'Piss off.'

'That's what you'd have been doing, for fucking years and years and years.' Dooley might have added more, but the major's torch beam flicked his way, and he caught its warning.

Andrea heard, but didn't listen. The conversations, the jokes, the arguments, all washed over her, she took no part and no interest in them. It wasn't contempt that made her ignore the men, not even fear that familiarity of any description might be interpreted as encouragement – to her they were simply not important.

In battle, yes, or when the discussion became serious and had to do with their work, then she listened, but not to this trivia. It was a constant surprise to her how men such as these, whose minds were full of thoughts of sex and drink and whose mouths spilled crude humour and obscenities, could when necessary weld instantly into a ruthlessly efficient fighting unit, capable of taking on an enemy force superior in numbers and machinery and defeating it or mauling it so badly it was left easy meat for others.

She had learnt something more about fighting from each of them. The sniper, Clarence, had taught her much and she'd absorbed all the skills he'd unknowingly passed on. And now she had tagged on to Dooley, from whom she was finding out all there was to know of hand-to-hand combat.

There was still so much to absorb, and there would be others among them who could teach her; but the hardest lesson of all would be the skills of command. Revell and Hyde both practised it as a fine art, yet in totally different ways. She hadn't yet decided which was best, but some day, one of them would also become her teacher.

'Shit, this don't leave us much to fight with if we tangle with a bunch of Ruskies.' York pulled out an M60 machine gun from the splintered remains of a case. Although obviously damaged, it looked a marginally more likely candidate for repair than any other retrieved so far.

'Cheer up.' Using his bare hands, Dooley partially straightened the thick tubular legs of a machine gun bipod, until they snapped, and he hurled them from him in disgust. 'If the cruds chop off your hands and feet, you can still pee on them and drown them.'

'With that great donger of yours, I reckon you could always club them to death.'

Andrea wasn't listening.

FIVE

From the top of the bell tower of the tiny church, Bombardier Cline could see much of the southern half of the island, by the light of the pale and watery dawn, though at times the snow made it indistinct as the last eddies of the dying wind pushed thick flurries around the building. The locations of the three sites for the launchers were just visible. The weather didn't matter. When the time came the radar and low-light TV would give him better eyes than his own with which to follow the progress of the Russian warships, and direct the rocket artillery's fire.

He gave a final twist to the clamp securing the miniature camera to the parapet. The instrument that had failed on test and that he'd just replaced was lying at his feet. The cold was numbing his hands, and had made him clumsy. Fear of dropping their last spare camera had made him work even slower.

There were other similar instruments set in trees along the shore, giving a healthy redundancy factor. Even if the Russians retaliated to their first salvo with a saturation counter-bombardment it was unlikely they could take out all the cameras, so long as they stuck to conventional warheads, that was. If the Communists got stroppy and used a low yield nuke, they'd be able to wipe this comparatively featureless island as clean as a billiard ball at one go.

It had been a good operation for Cline so far. He'd

survived the touchdown, found himself instantly elevated to command of the artillery contingent and felt he'd acquitted himself pretty well in the eyes of the Yank major and his horror-show NCO. All he had to do was stay sharp and he'd come through this with a promotion. That would be a handy short cut, save him a lot of tiresome face-stepping and back-stabbing. It was a real bugger, trying to make your mark, get noticed, among the mass of other sods in the battery who were keen to do the same thing. But now, now he had golden opportunity to save a lot of boot licking, he'd get that commission yet . . .

'You still fixing that?' Libby clambered up through the trap. 'I thought you said that was only a two-minute job. You'd better get back to the house and start checking the other circuits that have been hooked in, before the major comes after you.'

'Just who the hell do you think you're talking to?' In the armourer, Cline had recognised someone who might take a share of his glory, diminish its shine. It'd be best to put the bloke in his place early on, like now.

Unconcerned, Libby leant out and brushed snow from a ledge, watching the large soft lumps fall silently to the roof of the porch twenty feet below.

Stung by Libby's apparent indifference, Cline repeated his question, prodding him in the back to emphasise each word.

Slowly, as though reluctant to concern himself with the matter, Libby turned and faced the gunner. For a long moment, as the junior NCO bristled on tiptoe, Libby looked him up and down, adopting an expression of weary contempt as he completed the inspection.

'Shut up, you jumped-up little prat. While you've been piddling about with these lightweight peripherals, me and the others have been harnessed like a bloody dog-team hauling the bulk of your electronic gear to the house. The others are out there now, pulling ruddy great launchers and reload ammo fit to bust. I'm shagged, and I've not been made any happier by having the sarge send me chasing after you, like a bleeding company runner. So take this as fair warning, it's the only one you'll get. You ever lay a finger on me again and I'll snap it off, then shove you off here to see if you bounce.'

Despite the cold, colour rushed to Cline's cheeks, but the visual effect of his bottled indignation was spoilt by his inarticulate spluttering. 'You . . . I'll . . . I'll . . . have you . . . a charge . . . the major . . .'

'Oh, piss off.' Bored with the whole affair, Libby returned to contemplating the wall of the tower and the thin cable that ran from the camera, down its side, and was lost in the snow as it snaked away. He didn't watch Cline's angry departure, but he did allow himself a small smile, when shortly after the trapdoor slammed, he heard the bombardier's swearing as he slipped on the ladder.

He was glad to be alone, even for this brief moment. His hand delved deep into an inside pocket, and he pulled out the photograph. For the hundredth time he thought what a good idea it had been to have the copies made. This one was becoming very creased, the corners dog-eared, and the picture itself blurred by his dirty finger-prints. A breath on it and a quick rub with his cuff brought a marked improvement. He liked to be alone when he looked at it, liked to keep even her image to himself. And when he had the real thing once more, when he held Helga again, then Revell and Hyde and all the others and the Zone and the war, they could go to hell, they would have served his purpose.

The subdued throbbing of the generator outside could just be heard above the rapid clicking of the miniature printer. Switching off the terminal, York separated the flimsy strip and handed it to Revell.

'Are we in business yet?' His nose swollen to grotesque dimensions and spread across his face, Lieutenant Hogg spoke with a heavy nasal intonation. The blood that constantly trickled around his mouth, and dripped from his chin, had stained his anorak dark red.

'It's getting more promising. They've spotted a lot of

activity at Gdansk and a couple of other Polish ports where we can expect the escorts to come from. Still no firm figures, but I'm beginning to feel this breakout could be bigger than expected. A lot bigger.' Extracting a clip, Revell took one of the message strips that had been tapped out earlier. 'But at the moment I'm more concerned about this.'

Hogg took it, read, and attempted a whistle that failed and instead forced a large drop of blood from his nose. He wiped it away with the back of his glove. 'If the met boys have got this right, then the great-grandaddy of all cold fronts is heading our way. Says here temperatures of below minus thirty can be expected. Hell, now that is low. It'll freeze the nuts off the men.'

'It won't do Andrea a lot of good either, but there's other equipment I'm more concerned about. With the temperature dropping to that level we're bound to get an increased failure rate among the electronic gear, it's inevitable.' Through the largely glassless window Revell could see that the snow was definitely slackening. If the sky cleared then the mercury would plunge still further. 'How long before all three sites are ready, and we can do a complete system check for bugs? We can't be getting a true picture, testing each piece and link as it's installed.'

'Number one is ready now. Two will be at least a couple of hours yet. We could save time by stationing it closer in.'

'No, we're going for maximum dispersion within the perimeter of the intruder alarms. What about number three, the Lance.'

'With its trailer, that scales better than two tons, Major. Even if we hitch all the men to it, I can't see us shifting it far from the sledge. Once it's in place all we have to do is fix on the wings, survey the site and connect up. I reckon if we stick to our original plan we've another five hours' hard work, what with shifting all the reload rounds for the multiple launchers. Do we work during daylight?'

'Yes. No breaks until it's all done. I might have to think about it again if this cloud starts to thin, but for the time being it's full steam ahead, drive them hard.' Revell ticked off items on his check-list. 'What about the demolition charges?'

'I'll take care of them.' Hogg dabbed at his running nose. 'For the most part it's just a case of connecting the wires, but there's a fair bit of ground to cover, what with the remote decoy mortars and all. It'd be a help if I could have Libby. He knows what he's doing with that sort of thing.'

'Pick someone else. I'm not happy about our shortage of heavy weapons. We need at least one machine gun, and if anyone can salvage something from the junk pulled out from under that tractor, he can. Likewise I've got work here for York and Cline, otherwise you can take your pick.'

'The girl?'

Revell suspected an ulterior motive behind the lieutenant's query; he suspected anyone who took an interest in Andrea. 'Boris is with the working parties. He's safe enough out there with the other men, even Clarence. They've had an order to lay off, and they'll obey it. Andrea I can't be so sure of, so she stays here, giving a hand with the casualties.' That wasn't really how Revell wanted it. He'd far rather have had her here, in the control room with him, instead of upstairs. But he felt he had to display at least that much disinterest, even so, his thoughts constantly veered to her.

'Major, one of your men . . .'

'Shut the damned door.' Revell's shout was as loud as the crash with which Cline had thrown it open.

'Private Libby, he . . .'

'If you can't take care of it yourself, then learn to live with it. I'll be damned if I'm going to play nursemaid. Now if you've fixed that camera, get to work on the hook-ups to the launcher sites.'

Cline shut his mouth fast. Bugger, bugger, bugger: the realisation that he'd made a cock-up by complaining occurred to him forcibly. From now on he'd have to think first every time, and then be very smooth. Still, if he did his job by the book he should be able to paper over the

57

cracks he'd made in the image he'd been trying so hard to project. He'd have to, if he was going to turn the time spent on this harebrained mission to his advantage; and he would, or die in the attempt. Well maybe not die . . . but a neat and not too painful little wound would be in order . . .

The worst cases, those with multiple fractures or internal injuries, were laid on the bare floor. The other casualties sat propped against the wall, all around the room. All of them were encased in plastic-coated metal-foil survival bags, the shining cocoons helping them retain their precious body heat.

Libby had stuffed wads of paper into the broken panes of the single window, but it was only a gesture; there was scant difference between the temperature inside and outside the building. The day had brought no warmth.

As he worked to repair the salvaged weapons, his hands almost seemed to seize up with the cold. The metal of barrels and mechanisms stung and left cold-imprinted patterns on his palms and fingertips.

The men's breath hung in fine clouds before them, dispersing slowly in the light draughts. It was a perfect at-a-glance indicator as to the more serious cases; they could be recognised by the thin plume of vapour surrounding them, their weakened bodies barely being capable of shallow breaths. In two instances that vestige of white mist was the only sign that the men in question were still alive.

Gunner Fraser, his own head bandaged, moved quietly from man to man, tucking the cold limbs of the semi-conscious back inside their metallic wrapping, sometimes making a fractional adjustment to the position of a dressing or lighting a cigarette.

'Daft, isn't it.' Libby slid across to sit beside Andrea, as she watched the young medic's ceaseless fussing. 'At the moment it's the cold that's keeping some of the poor devils alive, slowing them down, giving their bodies a chance to start to cope with the damage, but in the end it'll be the cold that kills them. Why don't you give the kid a hand? That's why you're supposed to be up here. Go on, a pretty face is always good medicine. Surprise me and give them a treat, smile.'

She had never talked to Libby before. There had never been any need, and she would not have done so for any other reason. But now it was easier to talk than to try to ignore him, and she could turn the occasion to good use. 'Will the major order patrols, or are we to sit here and wait for trouble to come to us?'

'The intruder alarm perimeter is far enough out to give us fair warning if some of the natives or someone less friendly should stumble our way.'

'Then I do not know why we need to be here. Why not let the machines do it all? If they can find the enemy, why not give them the capability to kill also?'

'You don't mean that.' In spite of her German accent Libby had recognised the irony in her words. 'You love the killing. I've seen you doing it.'

'I do it well.'

'So does a nuclear bomb, but I wouldn't cuddle up to that either.'

'About the bomb I do not know, but there is no danger you would get the chance to do the other is there?' Taking her grenade-discharger fitted M16 with her, Andrea moved away and went to the window.

'And no bloody chance I'd want to.' Sod her, sod all bloody women, except for Helga. Sod 'em, sod 'em, sod 'em. When he deliberately moved to sit in the exact spot she'd occupied, he fancied he could feel something of her warmth. Sod her. Being near her, close to any woman, made his balls ache. He'd have to find a corner and work his frustration off in the same degrading way he always resorted to. Oh God, he did need a woman. He smiled to himself, a tight wry thing in the privacy of the grimy hands he rubbed over his face. He'd held out so long, but the next chance he got, he'd have to, he'd just have to. But he'd said that to himself the last time, and the time before

59

that, and so it had been for all of two years. Perhaps when, if, it actually came to it, he wouldn't be able to. Maybe lack of practice, or more likely his conscience, wouldn't let him. But it did no good to indulge in such speculations. The problem was now.

He casually stood up and went out to the tiny bathroom. Quietly and carefully, he pulled the door shut behind him.

'Fucking neutrals? I'd bomb the bloody lot of them, and all the shitty bleeding hearts and pacifists and fellow-travellers back home.'

The few daylight hours had gone, taking with them the low cloud that had offered some degree of concealment to their activities. In places, the first hard white points of light that were stars were already appearing.

Dooley turned from the kitchen window. With tight-clenched hands he was draining the last drop of warmth from the can of self-heating soup. 'I don't know how York does it. He reckons he's a decent cook, but somehow he can even screw up this muck.' His body ached, he could still feel where the harness straps had bitten into his shoulders and stripped the skin, even through his several thick layers of clothing. 'Why the hell should some po-faced pacifist shit be sitting at home, with a full table and a warm butt, while I'm stuck out here?'

'You're not the only one who wants to go home.' Burke had finished his soup and now crushed the double-skinned can and shied it into the sink.

'Who said anything about going home? I want the cruds out here with me, so I can show 'em just what it's like.' Dooley sent his can after Burke's. Aimed less accurately it bounced from the drainer and on to the floor, to be flattened under the big man's boot. 'It's the fucking neutrals I really hate, especially the fucking Frogs, I'd smear every last one of them.' He demonstrated his meaning by grinding the can hard into the boards.

Over in a corner, Clarence had built a nest of rags and

60

paper and burrowed into it with his sleeping bag, but the noise Dooley was making was preventing him from sleeping. 'Alright, so you don't like them, does your continuing tirade mean I'm not to get any rest? Now be a good idiot and be quiet for a while will you, six hours will do nicely, but I'll settle for two.' He pulled a smelly, dog hair-smothered, threadbare rug over his head. It didn't help, Dooley was like a record that had become stuck in a groove, going on and on. After a further five minutes Clarence could stand no more.

'That does it. I have to tolerate this ghastly war, you loathsome oafs, this stinking ruin, but I'll be damned if I'm going to put up with your simplistic all-embracing bigotry. Since when have you Americans been so fast off the mark in joining a war? Seems to me I remember a slight delay – of, what was it, three years? – before you came into the first World War. It took a reminder from the Japanese to get you into the second. You're only in this one because half your troops were stoked up on drugs when the balloon went pop, and the Ruskies clouted seven thousand of your men on the first day.'

It was not going to be that easy to get Dooley away from his pet subject, even using provocation of that magnitude. So determined was he not to be sidetracked, he virtually ignored the sniper's interruption except to glower in his direction and threateningly ball a huge fist. 'They're all the fucking same you know, the Swiss, the Swedes, the Finns, the Frogs; they're all a fuck sight more neutral towards the Commies than they are to us. It's only a couple of months since the Swiss shot down that Casevac transport. First thing I did when I heard about that was to go to a club I knew they used, to crack a few heads. When I got there I had to join a queue. Take the Swedes, smug bastards: free health care, free love and free coming and going for half the Red spys in Europe. And all the time they keep bleating about their neutrality while their factories keep supplying the fucking Ruskies with everything from telegraph poles to fur caps.'

'They have the highest suicide rate in the whole of Europe you know.'

'Let me know when it reaches a hundred per cent, I'll give a cheer.' Dooley turned to see who had come in, it was Boris. He took in the man's battered face and torn clothing, roughly held together by an assortment of improvised fasteners. 'I'm glad to see those bricks made a real mess of you. I couldn't be happier if it had happened to Burke. Nothing broken is there? No? What a pity!'

'You do not have to like me, I do not expect you to, but you should try to remember that we are fighting on the same side. Would you have spoken in the same way to Solzhenitsyn, or any of the other dissidents from the pre-war days?'

'There's the world of fucking difference between a dissident and a deserter. Those guys thought that way from the start, and said so. They didn't wait till they'd served a year in the Red Army, and had just been moved to the front before coming round to that way of thinking. I know your sort. Cruddy arse-licking party member while everything is going well in the motherland, then a whining shit-scared coward when your piddling little post at some factory suddenly comes off the exemption list.' Shoving the Russian roughly aside, Dooley stamped out of the room. In passing, he kicked two of the bottom rails from the stairs and booted their splintered remains ahead of him.

'You were lucky there, Boris.' Burke listened to the American's noisy progress to the control room. 'Friend Dooley gets really worked up when he's waiting to go into action, it ties him in knots. The only way he can let off steam is to lash out. If he'd swiped at you, you'd have snapped as easy as those rails.'

Boris sat on the corner of the wobbly pine table dominating the centre of the room. It creaked beneath him, but took his weight. Like the few other pieces of furniture remaining in the house it was too heavy and cumbersome for the owners to take with them in their rush to leave the place, and of too little value to be of interest to the looters who'd dared visit the island after the Swedish government had declared it a prohibited area on the outbreak of war, at the time of the first battles in the waters of the Kattegat.

'I should tell you, I was not a combat soldier with the Red Army. I was, I am a technician. That is all.' Boris took cigarette papers and a pinch of dark, almost black, tobacco from a stained leather pouch. He rolled the long shreds into the valley of white paper he made between thumb and forefinger, licked its edge and lit the finished cigarette with a lighter fashioned from a Russian 12.7mm heavy maching gun cartridge case. He toyed with it.

'And neither was I an intellectual, with the protection of the interest of the world's press. I am an ordinary Russian, not a party member. It took a long time for me to see, longer still even to summon up the courage to tell myself that what the Communists were doing to my country was terribly wrong. This lighter, it was produced, unofficially, at one of our second-line vehicle repair workshops, in East Germany. The men made and sold them so they would have the money to buy extra food. Their rations had been cut when their productivity fell. That happened because a senior officer, a member of the party of course, had diverted shipments of tools and spares to the black market. Without them they could not do their job.' Boris flicked the lighter on and off. It emitted a strong smell of petrol.

'The day after I bought this, the man who sold it to me was arrested, as were all the machinists and the junior officer in charge of the workshop. I think the machinists were sent to the northern Chinese border. The officer and the salesman were shot. There was no trial, not as you would know one. They were charged, gave their names, and were taken out. That in Russia is a trial.'

'For turning out a few crappy lighters?' Hyde took the lighter and examined it. 'Some of these parts have been cut by hand, you can see the marks of the saw. How many could they have made, ten, twenty?'

'The charge would have been sabotage of the Russian war effort. Anything which in the eyes of an official or an officer, if he is a party member, can be construed as

63

misuse of materials, is punishable by death. There is no appeal, in most cases there would not be the time unless there was some delay in mustering a firing squad, and usually there is one waiting. If they really wanted to get rid of you, then even wiping your nose on the sleeve of your uniform could provide the excuse. Usually they do not need one, but they have bureaucratic minds, and like to put a label to all that they do.' Accepting the lighter back, Boris returned it to his pocket. 'Your big friend was almost right. I had a secure position, actually it was at a small research centre. The pay was quite good and I rode with the tide, did nothing that would make ripples, attract attention to myself. I ignored what went on around me, even when an inoffensive colleague was arrested by the KGB. So long as I was untouched by it all, I closed my eyes, tolerated the shortages, pretended I did not see the privilege of the party members. But there is a time when these things can no longer be ignored.'

'Why the hell didn't you chuck them out years ago, you could have saved all this?' Sweeping his arm wide, Hyde took in the room, the island, the whole of the Zone.

Shoulders bowed, there was a weak attempt at a weary smile on Boris's bruised face. 'I was asked that by another British soldier during one of the interrogations after my desertion. My answer to you is, as it was to him, a question. Why did you not stand up to them years ago? Time after time the Free World let the Communists commit crimes that could have been prevented if the West had only stood up and shouted "enough", and backed the demand with determination and the threat of force. Afghanistan and Poland and all the others since, you sat back and watched. And worse, you kept supplying them with grain to feed their armies and the materials to make the pipelines that now keep their army in the field.

'The West has never understood that they are dealing with a bully, and when you are faced with a bully you do not hand over what he wants and then tie your hands behind your back, as the West did by not re-arming sooner. No, you refuse, and you wave the biggest stick

64

you can. For years your countries practised a cowardice that was matched only in its scope by the brutality and sadism of the Communists.'

'Who are you calling bloody cowards?' Forced on to the defensive by the accusations, Burke sought an answer. 'We did stand up to them, what do you think this war is all about?'

'Too little, and too late. Perhaps you would prefer I used the word appeasers, rather than cowards; but even an appeaser must take steps to protect himself when the bully's hands are at his throat and clawing for his eyes.'

Burke didn't bother to come back with another rebuttal. The Russian was much to close to what he personally saw as the truth. He felt cold. Unable to answer, he feigned interest in the rusting children's climbing frame in the garden, having to scrape frost from the dirty pane to see it.

'The snow has stopped.' Boris joined him at the window. Apart from a few places where it had drifted, the covering was only a foot or so deep. The branches of the trees at the back of the house had been swept clean of their light burden by the dying wind. Every bough and twig stood stark against the white backdrop. It was a two-dimensional landscape, like a pen and ink sketch on virgin parchment.

'Take a long look.' Hyde peered over the pair's shoulders. 'Next chance you get, it may have been remodelled by a few Commie surface to surface missiles and guns. Come to that, so might you.'

Running his tongue over the broken stumps of his front teeth, Boris felt the pulsing ache in his jaw and cheek. The process had already started.

5

SIX

'Are we ready for that floating Commie hardware yet?'
The room was dark, save for the glow from the screens.
Revell stood behind the bombardier and scrutinised the
complex assortment of electronic equipment set on various improvised tables and trestles in a crescent around
him.

'Computer is running the last tests now, Major. We
should get a green any moment, then we can start blowing
parts off those tubs whenever they appear.' Cline leant
forward and made a fractional adjustment to a dial. The
image on the main radar display sharpened.

A composite from three dishes, there was little to be
seen on it. To the west, the empty water of the Kattegat,
to the north the Swedish coastline tailed away towards
Norway and the open sea. To the south, the same coastal
strip led to the exit from the narrow waters of the Sound,
through which the Soviet warships must come. At twenty
miles, the neck of the opening was just visible at the
extreme limit of the low powered radar's range. A few
other islands scattered randomly along the coast completed the picture.

The tiny six-inch-diameter tube of the air-watch scanner
was a blank, and hopefully it would stay that way. Revell
was more interested in the image on the electro-optical
TV. It showed the Kattegat to be not as uncluttered as the
radar picture suggested. Although restricted in range by
their limited power source, the cameras were still able to

reach out all of six miles, picking out the stretch of sea at the limit of Sweden's territorial waters with perfect clarity. View after view, as Cline switched from camera to camera, showed the almost oily calm to be liberally scattered with variously sized slabs of floating ice. None were sufficiently thick to have registered yet, but in places they had come together to form floes a hundred yards across, and were growing more substantial all the time. Others were constantly being created.

'That should slow up any Swedish patrol boats.' After the way in which he'd almost queered it for himself earlier, Cline thought that things were beginning to go rather well – for him at least. His swift visual check of the components being unloaded from the sledge had revealed no apparent damage, and when all the gear had at last been set up, and he'd thrown the switch, every single status indicator had glowed an unbelievable green. A moment's worry, when the light indicating the condition of the standby batteries had flickered, had been quickly allayed by the discovery of a loose connection.

Without looking round, Cline knew the officer was still behind him, the ghost of his reflection showed on the hooded radar display. He didn't find it easy to communicate with Revell, talking to him was like throwing stones at a snow drift, made little impression, got no reaction. Still, it couldn't hurt to impress the stiff bugger at bit. Now was an opportune moment to enhance the good impression he must have already created by setting up and bringing the equipment into action single-handed. Cutting to the camera mounted on the church tower he zoomed in on two men trudging back to the house from their most northerly launcher site, number one, situated almost precisely in the centre of the island.

Revell could make out the faces of Lieutenant Hogg, and Ripper. Powdered snow plumed out from each footfall, and the men clutched empty demolition charge satchels that they hugged to their bodies as extra protection against the cold which made their breath hang in freezing clouds behind them.

Revell did acknowledge that the bombardier was good, but only to himself. He demanded that the men under his command do their job to the best of their ability, he expected no less, accepted no less, and doing it didn't warrant praise. In the gunner he recognised a climber, a man chasing promotion; in Cline's case chasing very hard. Well he was cocky enough already, he wasn't going to oblige Cline by inflating his ego still further. 'What's that?'

Cline snapped his attention back to the radar. A tiny green dot had sprung into existence just off the Swedish coast. It was moving perceptibly, and heading for their island. 'Patrol boat?'

'Not unless the Swedes are running some itty-bitty ones we don't know about. Try and get it on camera.' Revell craned closer, crowding the operator.

The snap-guess had been a bad one, Cline knew he should have allowed himself more time. On examination the blip obviously couldn't be anything bigger than a small yacht, twenty-foot maybe, although it was more likely a motor cruiser. The computer gave its speed as fifteen knots. 'I can't get it on camera, Major. None of them were mounted to cover the area between the island and the mainland. With the water too shallow for the big units we're expecting, it wasn't thought there'd be any need to.'

'Damn. Track it on the radar then. I want to know its precise landfall.' This was a complication Revell could have done without. Every possible contingency had been allowed for in the planning of the operation, but the probability of Swedish civilians visiting the island during the comparatively short period they were there had been calculated to be miniscule, and so his orders as to what to do in the event were brief and vague. Refugees in the Zone were one thing, neutral civilians on their own territory were quite another. No staff officer, even the greenest, was going to commit himself too definitely, in writing.

Short and in passing though his instruction had been on the subject, Revell remembered the nebulous phrase

69

'contact is to be avoided.' Avoided! Damn it, it looked like he had one or more Swedish civvies about to land in his lap.

There was no perceptible movement of air when the lieutenant and Ripper entered, but the drop in temperature was instantly noticeable. Body heat, the residue from the self-heating cans, and the miniscule amounts given off by the tubes had contrived to raise the reading in the downstairs rooms to several degrees above the outside. The stuffed and papered-over broken panes, a labour of love by York, had done much to help, even though the resulting filling of the windows had still further reduced the weak light during the all too brief day.

Blood continued to drip from Hogg's nose, and had soaked and frozen on his fur collar to create a dark spiked hedge. 'All the demolition charges are set, Major. Anytime you want, we can mangle the artillery beyond recognition and spread it around the island. If the Ruskies don't do it for us first.' He stamped and shuffled his feet. His toes hurt. Each one was a distinctively separate lump of marble that throbbed where it joined his flesh. 'What's it down to? It's just incredible out there.'

First brushing condensation from the dial, Cline checked the monitor. 'Forty below, and still dropping.'

'Get yourself some hot food. There's coffee and soup in the kitchen.' Noticing York rising from his seat, Revell motioned him back down, 'They can get their own. I want you to stay on the radio, start checking Swedish naval and coastguard frequencies. I want to know if that boat has so much as a CB set on board.'

Holding a near dead-straight course for the north of the island, the small trace had now covered half the distance. Cline let his mind riffle through a pack of speculations, but held back from offering any of them. He could smell the coffee being poured, could have done with another cup himself. Was it his imagination, or could he also feel its warmth? It was as if a narrow shaft of warmed air was wafting from the filled mugs and brushing past him. Again he inhaled the aroma, softer this time, the lieutenant was putting a dollop of condensed milk in his, having to gouge the barely fluid sweet white cream from the tin with his fingernails. Tearing himself away from the contemplation of the hot food, Cline turned back to the screen and forced himself to concentrate. The cold must be affecting his eyes, the screens looked dimmer, their pictures fuzzy and poorly defined. A hard blink and a second look brought no improvement, then he saw the dials. 'Major, we're losing . . .'

All three screens went blank and the glow faded from every dial and digital display. The room was plunged into darkness.

'Switch to batteries.' In the long moment of silence that followed the failure of the equipment, Revell became aware that he could no longer hear the drone of the generator.

The fact that it was pitch-black made no difference, Cline didn't need the beam from the torch that was turned towards the panels to find the controls he needed. using touch alone he pinpointed them as the brilliant pencil of light flashed into his face and forced him to close his eyes against its brightness. Slowly be opened them, faster as they registered that the harsh glare was gone, to find it being replaced by the soft sickly aura of the screens. 'Using all the systems, we can only run two hours on the batteries. If I cut the peripherals and only keep a couple of the principal functions, say the air-watch and surface radar, I can stretch it to five. We can always switch the others back in if we need to.'

'OK, do that. At least until we find what's the matter with the generator. Let the gunners out at the sites know what we're doing before you shut down. Tell them to double their guards.'

'That'll please them. Right now they'll be just starting to get nice and snug in their little tents.'

The voice was Burke's. Revel recognised the gruff tones, even though he couldn't see the man, somewhere at the back of the crowd that had come in the doorway. 'Let's see if a dose of work will cure that wagging tongue

71

of yours. You're the expert with engines, fix the generator. I want to know the moment you trace the fault. Sergeant Hyde!'

'Sir.'

The men parted to let the NCO through.

'We've got visitors.' A glance Revell took at the screen showed the unidentified craft still on course for the island. 'It's probably, almost certainly, civvies. I'd be happier if they didn't find us, but if they do trip over a launch site then I'll be very unhappy if we don't grab them before they get back to their boat. We can always figure out what to do with them later. I don't want them running off and squawking, and bringing half the Swedish navy and airforce down on us before we've had the chance to carry out our mission.'

'How many men shall I take?' Hyde began to fasten his snow-suit.

'I'll be taking them, Sergeant.'

It was Hogg who pushed to the front this time. A pillar of steam rose from his coffee. He stepped in front of the major and the vapour rising from the mug created a curtain between them.

'If you're figuring I can't see the state you're in behind that smokescreen, you're wrong. You've done enough, Lieutenant, you're in no condition to go out again for a while. When you've finished that get yourself upstairs to the medic, see if he can stop that bleeding, before you drain away.'

'When I'm in the open it dries up, I feel fine.'

'It doesn't dry up, it freezes up; and smokescreen or no smokescreen you don't look fine. You look like a victim in a horror movie.'

'Message coming in, Major.' Hand poised over the printout, York tore the strip off the instant the machine stopped. He leant back and stretched to hand it to Revell.

'This is it, we're in business. The latest satellite pictures show twelve major surface units moving out of Russian waters into the Baltic, and it looks like there's more to come. Twenty-five escort ships have moved from their

72

berths in Polish and East German ports. They're probably going to meet up inside Swedish territorial limits, and we can expect upward revisions on those figures.'

'Going to be a big party. I love parties.' Dooley's huge grin matched in width and display of teeth that which Hogg had permanently worn until the flying debris had made forming it painful.

'Find him some work, Sergeant. We could do with a few slit-trenches around the house, and check with Libby, see what he's managed to get into working order in the way of support weapons. What he hasn't fixed by now he'll have to leave.'

'What about the boat, Major? It'll be making landfall in the next ten minutes or so.' Hyde could see the chance of a little independent action slipping away from him. Bugger, and he'd been looking forward to the opportunity of operating as his own boss again, even if only for an hour or two. It would have been almost like the old days, before he'd joined the Special Combat Company, when he'd had his own tank-busting unit.

Hogg had not been slow to see the changed circumstances might be turned to his advantage. He jumped in. 'If you reckon the sergeant is fitter, Major, he'll be more use to you around here. Maybe I'll be better out of the way, strolling about keeping an eye on our late season tourists.'

'OK, you can take Clarence. Remember, avoid contact if it's humanly possible, and if it isn't be gentle. If we get bagged and interned simply for being here, that's one thing; getting hanged for what the Swedes would call murder is another.'

'They don't have a death penalty in Sweden.' Hogg didn't look up from the radar display. He was noting the precise location at which the trace of the boat suddenly merged with the island's, north-eastern coastline and ceased to exist as a separate entity on the screen.

'I bet they'd make an exception for us.' Passing through, a pick and shovel over his shoulder, Dooley was no longer smiling.

'What the hell are they doing?' Through the lens of the pocket image intensifier, Lieutenant Hogg kept constant watch on the comings and goings of the four men, as they moved among the broken walls of the old castle.

Using the night-scope on his rifle, Clarence had been watching as well. 'They've taken all the packs into the tower, but the sledge hasn't been unloaded yet, it's close by the arch leading in. It's a bit cold for a picnic.'

'Maybe it's an orgy. I heard the Swedes were big on that sort of thing. Hell, I wish we could use a radio, I know it doesn't look like these guys are going to roam about and stumble on our set-up, but my gut tells me there's something funny going on, and I sure would like to chew it over with the major.'

'I think one of them is a woman. The figure taking the box off the sledge . . . there . . . you see.'

'Either that's a man with a full pack stuffed down the front of his ski-suit, or like you say, it's female. That helps my orgy theory.'

'Not necessarily, Lieutenant.' Panning over the ruins, Clarence sought the other people from the boat. 'I've seen a few of the Swedish magazines Dooley buys: four men, four women, one woman and three monkeys, they'll do it with anything. That's nothing to go by.'

'There's one on the roof of the tower.' Hogg had to be careful not to breathe too heavily and to exhale towards the ground on which they lay among the leafless copse. Any other way would have fogged the lens, and produced a white cloud that might have betrayed their position. 'Is that an aerial he's rigging?'

'Could be, but we'd need to get closer to be certain.'

'Major Revell ought to know about this. You get word to him. I'll stay here and keep an eye on them.' Wiping his nose on the back of his mitten, Hogg winced at the pain it brought, but was pleased to see the flow of blood did at last seem to be slowing. The thick fabric of his glove was stiff with it, and he could feel where runs of blood had turned to ice on his face. Any fresh trickle either had to be wiped away immediately, or he needed to move his head from side to side in a gentle motion that prevented it from welding his face to his hood when it dripped sluggishly from his chin.

Pushing himself up on to his hands and knees, Clarence paused. 'You had better move around now and again, Lieutenant. The bottom must have dropped out of the thermometer. Cold has a way of creeping up on you.'

'I'm not about to let myself be turned into a popsicle when the best slice of action so far in the whole war is in the offing. Get word to the major, then we can get this sideshow sorted out and get down to the main business.'

Clarence didn't offer further argument or advice. Crouched low, and moving quietly through the powder-like snow, he started back to the house. The combination of snow on the ground and brilliantly sharp starlight provided sufficient illumination to light his way, but the absence of shadows made it impossible to see the prints they had made on the way out, and twice within a hundred yards, he missed his way. The cold was a very physical thing, plucking at him with needle-covered hands. Unable to measure it, he could only speculate on how far the temperature had now plunged. Recalling something he had read long ago, he made to spit. If his memory served, it would crackle when it touched the ground once the temperature had dropped below fifty degrees, but was it Fahrenheit or Centigrade? He couldn't be sure. The skin of his face was taut, his cheeks ached and he gave up the attempt to make spittle. For once he envied Hyde his ghastly face, at least the sergeant had no feeling in it. His eyes blinked hot tears that turned to ice droplets, and wiping them away added more discomfort, as in parting from his face the flakes and droplets seared his skin like freeze-branding irons.

The house was ahead, he could see movement close by it. Clarence felt relief, another hundred yards and then he'd be able to enjoy a cup of the disgusting, stomach-rotting coffee that York brewed. Strange, it wasn't getting any closer. Making the effort to bend in his bulky clothing he looked down. His legs weren't moving. That was silly, why had he stopped? It was only a little further, a hundred steps, but he couldn't get his legs to make one. There was a numbness in them that was spreading to the rest of his body. An overwhelming tiredness washed over him. He was locking solid, his strength had gone, sapped by the cold that crept through him, leeching his will. Just a few more paces, just a few. Why? Why a few more steps, where was he going? Silly to go on, why not just lie down, have a rest, sleep for a while. When he woke up he'd feel better, remember where . . . or was it what? It didn't matter, nothing mattered . . .

SEVEN

'Solid as a bloody rock.' Burke jabbed the stick into the fuel tank. 'Petrol's frozen. What do I do now, light a fire under it?'

'You do and the major will light one under you, if you don't blow yourself up first.' Dooley stopped work and looked up from his chest-deep excavation. 'The first three feet it's like going down through concrete, keeps you warm though.'

'But what the fuck do I do with this?' Not wishing to add to his work load, Burke resisted the strong temptation to kick the generator.

'You'll have to shift it inside, won't you?' Using pile-driver force Dooley drove his pick into the bottom of the trench, twisted it and then reached in to haul out a lump of half-frozen earth that must have weighed fifty pounds.

'You're joking. It took four of us to get the bloody thing here, and now the runners are welded to the shitty ground.'

'Why aren't you working, Burke?' Hood thrown back, his artificially precise hairline accentuating the featureless expanse of his face Hyde looked unreal, like a watery painting of a portrait by a child too immature to put in any but the simplest of details.

'Can't do any more outside, Sarge. It'll have to go inside if we're to have a chance of keeping it in action.'

'Alright, you heard him, Dooley, up out of your pit and give a hand here.'

'The major said I was to finish this before I did anything else.'

'You should have done already. Now if you'd pretended you were digging up one of the old women you like poking you'd have been down six feet already.'

'Heads I lose, tails I can't win.' Using the pick as a grappling iron, Dooley hauled himself from the hole.

'Give the runners a clout first, to break them free. A clout I said,' Hyde had only just ducked in time as the wildly swung pick whistled back between him and Burke, 'not an attempt at bloody wrecking it. Alright, we'll pull, you push.'

Ripper and Libby appeared and added their efforts. The heavy piece of equipment began to move, thrusting a wall of snow before it that constantly had to be shovelled aside.

'This weather is really something.' Almost sprawling as his foot slipped, Ripper prevented himself from going over by grabbing at Dooley.

'Gives you the urge to pull Dooley's pants down, does it?' The enjoyment Burke got from the scene was of short duration as he almost fell himself.

'Aw shut it. No, I mean the cold, it really gets to you. I reckon I'd have been a solid lump of ice by now, if I hadn't been too busy sweating, trying to get that foxhole dug.'

Standing back as Libby scuffed another bank of snow aside, Hyde looked out over the still countryside. 'It's not a night for standing around, that's for certain. Not that I'm likely to let you. Alright, now three more heaves and we'll have it lined up with the kitchen door. One last effort, and we're in.'

'I bet the lieutenant is regretting he was so fast to volunteer now. Him and Clarence must be wishing they were back here.'

Libby nodded agreement. 'You're probably right. No fun in being out there at the moment, no fun at all.'

'Radio batteries are OK, Major. My sets use only a

fraction of the juice those tubes do. Even if the generator is no good, used sparingly I can keep us in contact with the big outside world for two or three days.'

Revell had asked the question almost for the sake of something to do. He felt like the spider sitting at the centre of an intricately constructed web, waiting for his prey. The work was done, and the hours until the first of their Russian targets appeared would be long, and seem even longer. This wasn't the sort of war he liked. The real war was what you saw in the sights of your rifle, or felt at the end of a bayonet. Hanging around a command room, unable to move far from it, unable to do anything in it . . . that might be war for staff officers, for generals, it wasn't for him.

To fill in, to give himself something to do, he could have gone outside, lent a hand with shifting the generator, but the interference might not have gone down well with Hyde. He suspected that inside the British NCO there still lingered a residue of resentment at serving under an American officer, at having lost the independence he'd enjoyed as leader of a crack British anti-tank team.

There were times when Revell wished he was just a sergeant, with nothing more than his squad and himself to worry about. It'd be good just to get on with the fighting, to go out and do the damned job and to hell with the political consequences. While the Russians fought without constraints, his every action was hedged about by the need to avoid civilian casualties, or damage to property, or offence to other NATO partners. Rules, regulations guidelines . . . a Communist officer had none of those, he'd have an objective and perhaps a deadline and the fear of the consequences of failure . . . Revell could still hate the savagery with which the Soviet forces obtained their victories, while envying the freedom of action they were given to gain them. But it was a strange sort of freedom the Russian commanders enjoyed. Ten, twenty thousand civilian casualties didn't matter to a Warsaw Pact general as he drove his regiments towards their goal, but if he delayed by so much as an hour, then even if his primary objective was still achieved his removal was certain. A Russian's freedom was the freedom to butcher, to slaughter, but never to deviate from his observance of the strict orders he'd been given. It was that inflexibility that had cost the Communists outright victory at the start of the war, when none of their army commanders had dared even to attempt to plug the gaping holes in their advance caused by widespread mutinies among the East German and Polish units.

The NATO Staffs had rightly diagnosed that inflexible command structure as a weakness in the enemy, but had never got round to recognising as deadly a failing in their own strategy. When faced with an opponent prepared to resort to every dirty trick, to employ the full range of horrific modern weapons of mass destruction, half-measures to contain them could only resort in half-victories, or more usually half-defeats.

That Lance missile, standing out in the snow waiting for him to transmit the coded command to commence its near instantaneous firing sequence and launch, was a good example of NATO's, or rather the West's mentality. Four separately targeted warheads nestled within the sharp nose of the missile. Their fuses precisely pre-set, they would detonate above a Swedish Air Force base, a vital hydroelectric power station, a coastal patrol craft complex and a garrison town. Spectacular though their kiloton warheads would be, that would be the limit of their effectiveness.

It was a half-measure. If the Swedish parliament was as nervous as the Western analysts believed, and if it was still in permanent session at that time, it was possible it might over-react, declare on the NATO side before all the facts were gathered and the discovery made that in reality no damage had been suffered. But it was more likely to do what it had been doing for two years, dither and talk and let the moment pass in frightened and confused indecision. Then the West's only hope would be that a local commander with a few coast defence missiles under his control might not wait for orders, might retaliate instantly to what he saw as a Russian bombardment preceding an assault.

What a way to fight a damned war . . .!

York and Cline were preoccupied with their respective electronic equipment. Outside, Revell could hear Hyde exhorting the men to greater effort. The generator being bumped against the wall, and the shout of someone whose fingers were between the two. From upstairs came the rare loud groan of one of their casualities. Andrea was up there . . . he should go and see how the injured were faring, he hadn't checked on them for several hours . . .

'Go down and get yourself a coffee. I'll be up here for a while.'

The young gunner-medic made a fussy last adjustment to the bandage he'd been replacing, then went out. His footsteps echoed back to Revell from the uncarpeted stairs.

It was darker than the fire-control room. Only white or very light coloured objects stood out in the breath-misted gloom. Bandages were clearly visible, as were the pale hands and faces of the men wrapped in their life preserving silver chrysalises. The hard rasping breathing of a chest case was the only audible sound.

Andrea was over on the far side of the room, struggling to fully fasten the zip of a silver cocoon. Carefully, Revell stepped between the bodies to go and help her.

'It is done.' With a last effort Andrea sealed the body into its crinkling shroud before Revell reached her. 'He is the first, others will follow. I think that one is next.'

Revell followed her pointing finger to where a scrap of white cloth blended imperceptibly into the deadly pallor of a face it didn't entirely cover. 'I don't know how he's lasted this long. He lost a lot of blood when his arm was taken off. I'll have the body moved as soon as the men have finished shifting the generator.' There were other matters Revell wanted to talk about with her, but in the darkness he couldn't be sure all of the casualties were sleeping.

6

He'd never managed to be alone with her for more than a few moments. Not that he'd ever been really conscious of her manipulating it that way, but on reflection he felt sure that she had. Never very communicative, she immediately stiffened and backed away from contact with any man she sensed showing an interest in her. With her looks, that kept her perpetually on her guard. The skills she displayed at holding men at a distance, and generally taking care of herself, were considerable; the way she managed Dooley was ample proof. Revell couldn't tell whether the big man got anything from the relationship, other than having, and enjoying, the prestige of having her near. Several savage slapdowns he'd received in public suggested there was less than truth in many, perhaps all, of his private boasts.

Damn it, Revell had never felt so protective towards any woman, not since the early days of his marriage to the bitch, and that had soon been beaten out of him by spite and neglect and contempt. And now he had this irrational urge to take Andrea under his wing, a woman more able to take care of herself than any other he'd ever known. It was stupid, irrational, when he'd made up his mind to treat her no differently from any of the men. And it was dangerous as well. Dangerous because his preoccupation with her could affect the efficient running of the unit, because it could cost some or all of them their lives unless he could come to terms with it.

From where it lay on top of a pile of rags, Andrea picked up her scarred and chipped M16. The fat tube of the grenade-launcher below the barrel gave it a clumsy and ill-balanced look. 'When do I use this? I am not a nurse, this is not where I belong.'

'Perhaps you won't need to. If the mission goes according to plan then we do the job and get out without firing anything but the heavy artillery. Command won't be too happy if we start a big fire-fight with Swedish patrols. Why do you think they sent such a small escort group, with so few support weapons? It's so that if we do start trouble we can't cause too much of it.'

'The West does not deserve to win this war.' Andrea turned to the window, and stared out. 'They expect their soldiers to die, but do not want them to win.'

'That about says it.' Revell moved to stand beside her. He liked her clipped German accent. Her manner was sharp, he could visualise an affair with her being very one-sided. She would dominate any man, he imagined her being very strict, very severe . . . No, he backed away from the thought. That was a speculative road he didn't like to travel. There was a darkness at its end he didn't care to pierce, for fear of what he might discover about himself.

The snow covering the island gave the landscape a strangely two-tone, two-dimensional effect. There were no greys, no shadings to give depth or texture to any object. After a few moments the weird monotony of the scene began to play tricks with his eyes. A log, or it might have been a rock protruding above the snow, almost seemed to be moving. Of course it couldn't be, there was nothing alive out there, God had shut shop for the winter, even Clarence would find nothing to kill . . .

'Come on.' Revell didn't think to, didn't have time to, define what prompted him to jump and stride over the close-packed casualities; but intuition or some sixth sense told him that shapeless dark hummock he'd dismissed as a log was one of his men. His boot rapped against an improvised splint and elicited a groan from the man he'd almost stepped on, then with Andrea close behind he was out of the room and taking the stairs three at a time. He was shouting for the medic even as he raced for the front door.

At ground level everything looked very different, but he had a bearing and snow sprayed ahead of him as he ran. There was an icy feeling inside him that had nothing to do with the cold.

'The lieutenant thought you ought to know about it.' There was an intense cramping pain in Clarence's fingers and toes as circulation gradually returned. He could feel the soup in his stomach radiating warmth through his body, and breathed in the steam that rose from the can he held clumsily between clenched fists, not feeling the hot metal burning into his blue knuckles.

'And that was all you saw? Just three men and a woman moving supplies of some sort into the old tower.'

'We tracked them from the boat. It looked like an old wreck, as if it shouldn't still be afloat, but it was, and its motor sounded alright. After they'd got out of sight we took a chance and had a look inside. We had to give them a bit of a start, there's not much cover up that end of the island.'

'Did you find anything?'

'Nothing. I got the impression the hull and mechanics had been well maintained and the rest of it allowed to go to hell. Funny, you'd think anyone who owned a big yacht would have taken care of it.'

'Can't get the petrol, no point.' Hyde had been listening. 'There must be thousands of beautiful boats rotting away along this coast.'

'But then why look after the engine, why keep it in good running order? Sergeant, take Ripper and two others and find Lieutenant Hogg. If he hasn't got positive proof that bunch are harmless – I don't know, maybe a group from a university or something – then go in and grab them. Something about that set-up isn't right, and I want to know what.'

'I'm getting something, Major.' York settled his headphones more snugly. 'This is weird. My gear isn't directional so I can't tell where, but I'd say somebody on this island is transmitting.'

'What language?' Revell picked up the spare headset, plugged in and held it to his ear.

'Swedish. Shit, it's gone.' After a minute spent trying every frequency, York took off the headphones. 'Not there any more.'

'On your way, Sergeant. We both know where that must have been coming from. Tell Lieutenant Hogg to take whatever action he has to, I want an answer to this damned riddle, and fast.' It wasn't until he'd turned round that Revell saw who Hyde had selected to go with him beside Ripper. Dooley and Andrea were pulling up the hoods of their snow-suits. It was an intelligent choice he couldn't argue with, the pair worked well together. Clarence wasn't fit to go anywhere for the time being, he wasn't prepared to trust their Russian that far from his sight, and Libby and Burke were busy with the generator.

The door closed behind the trio, and Revell resisted an urge to rush to it and call Andrea back, to replace her with Libby. There was a better than evens chance he was soon going to make a fool of himself over her, unless he made a greater attempt to curb his feelings, or at least the emotions they gave rise to. A loud crash from the kitchen broke into his thoughts, which were then swept aside by the voluble swearing that followed the heavy metallic noise.

'You fucking clumsy shit bag. First you fucking near rupture me and chop my fingers off when we were lugging the bleeding thing in here, now you're trying to break me sodding toes.'

Libby's low-key reply to Burke's tirade wasn't audible in the control room. Revell heard their driver's follow-up, then the argument petered out into various angry mutterings.

Cline was making the routine contact with the gunners at the various launch sites, meticulously logging each call, looking at his watch each time and noting the exact minute and second. He cleared down the last connection, rubbed his eyes, squared his pencil and notebook, polished the air-watch radar screen, pulled his rickety leatherette-covered dining chair closer and checked the surface radar display.

'Er, Major. I have a second unidentified trace, a vessel.'

'Another launch?'

'Er, no, sir. This is in the thirteen to eighteen thousand ton class, and it's coming out of the Sound.'

'That's not possible, the Ruskie warships won't reach

there for another ten hours according to the last satellite update.' There was an image. It had crept into existence as a fuzzy green ovoid at the bottom of the screen. The computer quietly hummed to itself as it waited for sufficient data to calculate she ship's course and speed.

'Could it be a cargo boat, a small tanker maybe?' Cline jotted the event down in the inevitable notebook.

'No, no chance. The Swedes stopped all their coastal traffic a week ago, and all the other neutrals have sense enough to know this is not the time to sail. Whatever that is, it's Russian. Punch up a course prediction.' Revell watched a broken green line sprout and grow from the blip to skim past their island. 'So, it's big, it isn't friendly, and it's coming straight at us.'

EIGHT

'It's the right size for a Moskva class anti-submarine cruiser.' It was too good an opportunity to miss, Cline used it to show off some of his knowledge. 'Only I thought those things never moved without a swarm of escorts.'

'Size is about the only thing that is right. They only built two of those brutes, *Leningrad* is somewhere in the Med, *Moskva* herself is at the bottom of the North Atlantic.' Again Revell looked at the printout of information endlessly and repeatedly marching along the base of the screen. 'The damned thing's speed is what's got me foxed. I expected those surface units to come out of the Sound going hell for leather, this ship is doing barely eighteen knots. How long before we get it on visual?'

'Forty-three minutes, at present speed.'

'Good, we should have the generator functioning again by then, if Burke can prevent it from making more batches of petrol cubes.'

Cline decided to have a last try. 'Could it be a decoy, to flush us out?'

In his mind Revell had already considered and dismissed such a possibility. 'I don't doubt the Ruskies have got a few time-worn hulks they might risk for that purpose, but their admiral's have been a bit short on subtlety and initiative lately. Anyway, the loss of the tonnage might not matter to them, but they're short on experienced ratings and artificers. Their lives wouldn't matter, but their skills would take time to replace. No, whatever that is, we can take it at face value.' He turned to York, who'd been listening to the exchange, and rather enjoying the shooting down of the bombardier's pet theories. 'Get on to Command, ask them what it is.'

While the message was tapped in, and the buttons pressed to encode, scramble and condense the text for a transmission of barely a second's duration, via satellite, to Command HQ, Revell watched the imperceptibly moving trace. The wait was surprisingly short.

A burst of muted chatter from the printer, and York tore off the strip it disgorged and handed it to the officer.

'Either they don't believe us, or they haven't done their homework. We'll risk another transmission. Tell them we've got a blip that's big and real and heading our way. I want to know of any Warsaw Pact vessel of that size that's been reported anywhere between here and Bornholm in the last ten days. The damned ship can't have materialised out of nowhere.'

The wait was longer this time, and when the printer did come to life it did so fitfully, as though the information from the retrieval system the other end was feeding the various pieces of information to them one bit at a time, as it unearthed them in its comprehensive banks.

Four vessels were listed on the ribbon of paper that Revell almost snatched from York. The facts as they were presented were cryptically stark, but his memory, supplementing that of the computer, filled in the ugly detail. Two were tankers, the survivors of a convoy of fifteen that had run the gauntlet of NATO air-attacks and long-range bombardment, from an East German port to the Russian and Hungarian forces occupying the Danish islands. Both had been sunk on the return journey, along with the last of their corvette and frigate escorts. The third vessel on the short list was the Polish floating crane VK27, which had been towed to Copenhagen to speed the clearance of the last of the scuttled British and Dutch cargo ships from the harbour.

Number four, the last, was a Polish grain carrier, whose crew had loaded it with family and friends and attempted to reach the West. They had failed when the ship, crippled by a NATO mine and dead in the water, had been sunk by shore-based Russian aircraft. NATO naval units, too late on the scene, had only been able to take bodies from the water, after beating off the Migs that had spent an hour repeatedly strafing the lifeboats full of women and children. Revell's mind was crammed with such facts, an endless catalogue of horror and brutality. No wonder the press back home had stopped reporting every incident of that type committed by the Communists. After a while it had become overwhelming, and the people had started to disbelieve. So now they got a ration, only one or two such stories a week, and those chosen not for their truth, but for their variety and plausibility. The worst they never heard; would never have believed.

Crumpling up the paper the major balled it in his fist and hurled it into a far corner. 'According to the Staff and their all-knowing computer we have a ghost ship coming at us.'

'I don't believe in ghosts, Major, not ones that register on radar. Who ever heard of thirteen thousand tons of ectoplasm?'

'Let's get Boris in here, he can start to earn his keep properly.' While York went to fetch the Russian, Revell stepped outside. In the house it was cold enough, but in the open . . . like jumping into freezing water, it took his breath away. He'd told Cline to cover the temperature monitor. Now it had gone so low that it could only be of academic interest. It would have been good to take a deep breath, flush the smell of petrol and oil from his lungs, but the air was so sharp, so biting and numbing that he did it by degrees, exhaling and inhaling slowly through pursed lips to warm the air before it reached down into his body.

Within the house the generator coughed and spluttered into reluctant life, to expire a moment later. Second and third attempts to start it met with no success and were followed by swearing from Burke.

Revell thought of the gunners huddled in their tents close by their charges. They'd been marvellous so far, the survivors doing the work of twice their number. What they'd be going through out there would be a further hard test of their mettle. They knew only as much as they could glean from the brief periodic exchanges over the land lines. Apart from that fragile contact with the house the artillery men were totally on their own, as they would be when the action started. Then they would have to leap from chilled lethargy into instant sweating action, traversing and elevating the launchers in accordance with the instructions that would flash on to the 'black boxes' attached to each one. Then, when the massive projectiles had gone screaming on their way, in expectation of a counterstrike against which they'd have virtually no protection, they would have to hurriedly reload and go through the whole mad process again, and again, until an enemy missile registered on their site, or no more targets were presented.

They, and Revell, knew which was by far the most likely alternative. Mobility was the artillery's only protection on the modern battlefield, and the towed launchers had none without the tractor. Enemy radar would pick up the rockets in flight and, by computing their path, track back along to their place of origin. What happened then depended only on the armaments of the vessel involved.

The command centre at the house shared the danger, not simply because of the Russian tactic of blanket retaliation, but because of the mass of electronic emanations which would come from it at the height of the battle. On the latest detector equipment it would stand out like a flashing sign in the frozen landscape. Since most of the enemy ships were brand-new or fresh from extensive refits, they would have that latest equipment and the weapons systems to go with them.

'That ghost ship is coming into range of our cameras. Shall I switch on now, Major?' Cline let his hand hover over the controls.

'Give it a moment longer. Another mile or so and we'll

get better definition. No point in wasting juice and straining our eyes trying to make out a blur.' In the kitchen Revell could hear Burke's successive attempts to start the generator. Each time the recalcitrant engine would turn over for a few seconds, then fade, sometimes with a subdued fart-like backfire. 'OK, let's see it now.'

'There it is.' With the co-ordinates already supplied and fed in from the radar, Cline's screen immediately picked up the ship. 'Range is five miles, and it's reducing speed. Down to ten knots, Major, and still slowing.'

Revell examined the angular grey outline of the amphibious warfare vessel. Every detail showed clearly, from the 76mm mount on the raised bow, to the pennant flying from the rear of the stern helicopter pad. The number '120' was painted large, in white, on the bow aft of the stowed anchor. He knew the number, and knew that Cline's frantic thumbing through identification lists would not find it, but he needed to confirm what was much stronger than a suspicion. 'Boris, come here. Can you make out the name, it's just below the rear platform?'

Taking a pair of wire-framed bifocals from a zipped pocket, the Russian laboriously hooked them to his ears, then peered over the top of them at the screen. Very slowly he raised and lowered his head to take advantage of the different strength lenses in turn. 'The rust does not make it easy, but it looks like *Ivan Rogov*.'

'He's got it wrong, must have.' Cline had failed to find the ship listed, even on the stapled update page he'd added shortly before leaving Bremen. 'We sent that tub to the bottom four months ago. I saw it on the newsreels.'

'I saw that footage too, she took half a dozen hits off Copenhagen, very spectacular, but unless we're about to revise our disbelief in ghosts, that is the *Rogov*.' Revell could see the bow wave and white water created by the ship's passage was diminishing. 'Alright, Boris, get back to your station. Pick up what you can. I want to know what the hell that battered scow is doing here.'

At three miles, the ship stopped in the water and dropped anchor. There was a plume of mixed spray and broken ice as the chain-towing metal struck a floe. Several areas of the vessel had a patched and repaired appearance, as if the work done on her had been finished in a hurry. Large sections were painted only in primer.

'What the hell is an LPD doing in these parts? Landing platform docks carry a battalion of marines and forty tanks or trucks. Why the hell would they be stopping here? This is the wrong place to start an invasion of Sweden.'

'Try this for an answer, Major.' Reading the strip as it came from the printer, York hesitated before tearing it off and handing it over to the officer. 'I don't think you're going to like it.'

'Has Sweden declared on Russia's side?'

'Not yet, Bombardier, not yet.' Reading and re-reading the signal didn't alter its text, Revell did it to savour the irony. All the care that NATO Command had put into choosing this island, this rather than any other. 'No, they haven't gone through the charade of signing a "communal defence pact", but as far as we're concerned they might just as well have done. The Swedes have agreed to the Russians setting up a monitoring and tracking station on their west coast. They've said they can have the use of an island; guess which one?'

'Shit, the bastards have got him.' The lieutenant's body was stiff as a board and frozen to the ground. Dooley had to use a lot of force to turn it over.

'No, it weren't them.' Hyde put his gloved hand on Hogg's face, and felt his fingers slide across the smooth mask of iced blood that encased the lower half of his features. 'He stayed still for too long, you can't afford to do that out here.' Picking up a handful of the loose snow he covered the lieutenant's face, then prised the Colt commando sub-machine gun from his locked grasp, and pushed it into a drift at the base of a clump of birch.

'Come on, there's still work to be done.' Hyde had to shove Dooley, who was mesmerised by the corpse.

'Jesus, what a way to go.' He began to move as Hyde prodded him forward. 'I heard of blokes choking on their own blood after getting their schnozzles bust in a fight, but I ain't never seen nothing like that.'

'Ah don't know all the ways there are to die in a war, yet,' Ripper was keeping pace alongside Andrea, but had given up trying to start a conversation with her, irritable with the smirks Dooley gave him at each rebuff. 'But we had a couple of feuds going in my valley, and the ideas some of those guys tried on each other, you just wouldn't believe it. There was this good ol' boy, a Jenkins I think, he made for the can after a longish session in the back room. He sure must have had a few beers inside him 'cause he was in a heck of a hurry, and he weren't looking what he were doing. And he sure should have been, on account of the fact he'd got in a lucky shot the week before and peppered Grandaddy Jepson with better than a couple a hundred pieces of buckshot. Anyhow, this good ol' boy makes it to the can, whips out his peashooter and starts a-hosing fit to bust. Only trouble is some guy had emptied the bucket and put a chunk of sodium in it. You know what happens when sodium and water mix, well it must have been a big chunk, and I reckon it reacted much the same to a dousing in processed beer. They found the roof of the shed in the next county, and the preacher's cat were seen chewing on what looked mighty like a charcoal grilled peashooter. Mangy brute swallowed it when he saw he were about to lose it, so we never knew for sure. That was the only part of the good ol' boy that were ever seen again.'

'Touching, not to say unbelievable.' Leading the group into a shallow depression close to the ruins of an outer wall, Hyde gestured the need for silence.' We could sit here all night, trying to figure where all four of them are. My bet is they're in the tower. We'll work on that assumption. I want minimum casualties, minimum noise. Better still, none of either.'

'There is only the one way in, and the door looks thick and heavy.' The bayonet that Andrea was fitting to her

93

rifle was burnished to a mirror finish, in imitation of Dooley's. 'A grenade would be a more certain way of opening it, or do you think they will be kind and let us in if we knock politely and say please?'

'That door is thick and heavy and old, very old. Whatever rusted fastening is holding it, I'm gambling our human battering-ram here is stronger.'

Andrea looked as if she might argue with the sergeant, but she didn't, and returned the high explosive grenade to the pouch on her belt.

'Let's go.' Hyde stood up and started forward. 'Fan out until we reach the arch, then we take it at the run. You'll lead, Dooley.'

'Gee, thanks, Sarge. I'm the biggest target.'

'You're the biggest shield as well.' Ripper would have added more, but Hyde had heard the whisper, and silenced any follow-up with a growl that brought no movement to his dead face.

Making no sound, they moved towards the tower that stood jagged-topped above the remains of walls about its base. Here and there a portion of carved stonework survived, jutting from frost-sintered masonry. A few large blocks, fallen from long-vanished vaulted roofs, littered the ground and turned the tracks the four left behind them into a pattern of weaving gash-like depressions.

Dooley checked the others were with him, before stepping through the arch immediately before the door. He was almost close enough to reach out and touch the weather-pitted, iron-bound planks, was gathering himself for a shoulder-charge, when it swung open.

A spectrum of expressions flickered over the face of the middle-aged man who opened the door. Fear was instantly changed to surprise that was fast transformed into a broad smile which a hand extended to endorse, then those were swept away as he caught sight of the NATO weapons the group carried, and fear blended with anger returned as he attempted to slam the door and began to shout a warning.

Deciding the same tactics could still be of service,

Dooley made his shoulder-charge, crashing into the retreating man and going down with him as he stumbled backwards.

Two oil-lamps lit the bare walled ground floor room, and by their light, Ripper, last of the four to enter, saw that it was already over. Dooley was disentangling himself from a weakly struggling figure on the paved floor, Andrea was threatening a bearded man seated at a radio, who was not being swift enough in raising his hands, and Sergeant Hyde was covering a surly young blond male who had been trying to reach a powerful hunting rifle propped against a wall.

Keyed up, feeling cheated at not having taken part in the real action, Ripper reacted without thinking when he heard a noise in the doorway behind him. Whirling round, he lunged with his bayonet at the large figure turning to run, saw the long blade plunge in through the silky fabric of a yellow ski-suit, and felt it part and slice into the flesh beneath. Instantly, his rifle was dragged down, almost from his hands, as the victim slowly collapsed without uttering a sound.

Smeared red, the blade slid out, as the woman turned her face up to him and slumped to a sitting position in the doorway.

NINE

'I don't know what this lot is for, but smash it anyway.'
Hyde stood back as Dooley set to work destroying the
radio equipment, using the hunting rifle as a sledgehammer. 'Soon as that's done, seeing as how you've warmed
yourself nicely, go outside and scout around for any more
gear they may have stashed.'

None of their prisoners had spoken, or made any move to
intervene when Andrea had grabbed the woman by the hood
of her ski-suit and dragged her into the middle of the room,
before closing the door. Hyde's brief questioning had failed
to elicit any response from them either, save for an
accentuating of the curled-lipped arrogance of the young
man. That had been sufficient to tell him that one of the
group at least understood English, and now Hyde had a
second go.

'Do you have a first-aid kit? Bandages? Do you have
bandages? Oh, I'm wasting my fucking time with this bunch.
Andrea, keep them covered. Ripper, give me a hand here.'

Close to, the woman was older than he'd at first thought,
well into her forties and looking it, though the pain she was in
was probably not doing much for her. She lay on her back.
Hyde brushed aside the weak attempt she made to stop him,
and unzipped her suit. Heavy breasts, unrestrained by a
brassière, sagged sideways but still made appreciable
mounds through her several layers of clothing. 'Not much
blood, can't find the sodding entry point, where did you get
her?'

Tentatively Ripper bent down, gingerly pulled her arm away, and indicated an almost invisible tear in the material just above her thick waist.

For the first time she made a noise as Hyde half-turned her to pull the suit off the shoulder. It was too tight a fit, and instead he had the American hold her, while he inserted his fingers in the rent and tore the tough synthetic fabric. She gave a small bleating cry as he shoved her arm out of the way so that it flopped across her breasts, and scuffed up her jumper to expose the wound.

'Very neat.' Hyde examined the slim cut. 'If we could fix bodies the way we can clothes, this would be a good case for invisible mending. Keep her on her side.'

'I didn't know she was behind me, I mean I didn't know it was a woman.'

'What's that got to do with it? If it would have been right to do it to a man, why's it wrong to do it to her?' Hyde took a small automatic pistol, and a clip of ammunition from a pocket which moving her had revealed. 'I'm starting to think this crowd are not your standard tourists. Give me your field-dressing, then go through their things, search every pack and . . .' Hyde winced at the amount of crashing and banging Dooley was managing to produce as he thoroughly demolished the radio and rifle, ' . . . and tell that big ape I said to destroy them, not atomise them. He can do the other job I gave him.'

With a final tremendous blow that ripped the front panel from the radio and the butt from the rifle, Dooley finished, and took a surreptitious peek at the woman's breasts, pushed up and together by the folds of clothing tucked beneath them.

'Nice pair of tits. Think they'll, she'll, make it?'

'Who knows, she's in shock, maybe.' As the closing door sent a flurry of flakes across the floor of the room, Hyde smoothed the tapes securing the wad of absorbent dressing, pulled the woman's thick roll-necked sweater down and tucked it into the ski-suit as best he could. The additional bulk beneath the suit, added to the woman's ample proportions, prevented him from fastening it completely. He hauled her to the wall near their other captives, and propped her against it. She fainted as he did so.

'Nothing much in these, Sarge.' Picking up the last of the packs, Ripper emptied them on to the floor and scattered the contents with the toe of his boot. 'Mostly food and spare clothing. Found these though.' He held out a small hammer and half-empty cellophane pack of masonry studs. 'This is what they used to fasten those blackout curtains.'

'They came prepared for just about everything.' Hyde kicked the remains of the radio, and it tumbled to the feet of the man Dooley had flattened. He was nursing his shoulder and his face was bruised, he jumped, misinterpreting Hyde's action and taking it as a threat.

That would be the one to work on to get information. Sergeant Hyde had seen the same symptoms displayed before . . . the civilian's nerve had gone. The tensions surrounding whatever it was their party were involved in, the assault, and the wounding of the woman had combined to reduce him to a shivering, cringing wreck.

'Soon as Dooley's back we'll move. I'm beginning to get a glimmering of what's going on here. I don't know what the details are, but it's obviously part of some larger set-up, and I don't want us being caught in the middle of somebody else's grand plan.'

'What do you reckon they're up to then, Sarge?'

'Are you really so stupid?' Andrea's tone dripped contempt for Ripper's innocent question. 'Do you really not know what these worms are?' While she spoke her eyes stayed locked on the prisoners, the barrel of her rifle slowly panning back and forth across the group. 'In your own country there was a left wing orchestrated cry of "witch hunt" every time a man with intelligence, with integrity tried to weed them out. In Britain that tactic was rarely needed to protect them. Their type were able to worm their way into the highest places in the government and the administration, even into the secret services, where still that country suffers from the harm they did.

These are Communists, the lowest form of animal life, who sell their country for money, or the promise of power. We should finish them now.'

'No you bloody don't, you're not appointing yourself chief executioner again, not while I'm leading this patrol.' Hyde kept a casual grip on his rifle, but held it so that he could bring it to his hip and fire in an instant. 'The major wants this lot, and I'm not about to go back without them. We'll let him do the judge and jury bit.'

'What else could they be, why else would they be here?' She momentarily turned her head towards Hyde, and her dark eyes flashed frustration and fury.

'I don't know, perhaps they are Commies. We'll find out when we get them back to the house, until then . . .'

'Tanks . . .' Dooley threw open the door, and stood clutching his chest as he gasped for breath, '. . . fucking Russian tanks, two of the buggers, with infantry, coming this way.'

'Get those lights out. Put the woman on that little sledge, move . . .' Hyde never got to finish the sentence.

As Ripper went to pick up the woman, he momentarily blocked Andrea's view of the three male prisoners. The young blond grabbed the opportunity and dashed for the door. About to extinguish a light, Dooley wasn't close enough to intercept, and instead he slammed the door. It caught the blond on his shin, thigh, and head and there was an ugly sickening crunch as the heavy wood made contact and swept him aside. The Swede was spun around by the impact and thrown into the wall. Dazed by the blow, he didn't even have time to use a hand to protect his face.

The other two men were easily dissuaded from a half-hearted attempt to follow him by the aggressive and threatening gesture Andrea made with her M16. They meekly allowed themselves to be herded from the tower, supporting their dazed and bleeding comrade, at the tip of her bayonet.

Hyde was last to leave and trailed behind the others, scuffing a confusing riot of marks into the snow to disguise their tracks, as they made for a clump of trees three hundred yards to the south. As they reached it, headlamps and powerful torches were throwing long pencil beams of yellow light across the snow, illuminating the castle's outer walls.

'Do you need further proof?' Handing over responsibility for their captives to Dooley, Andrea knelt beside the sergeant and watched the procession of wheeled and tracked Soviet army vehicles winding up from the sea towards the ruins. Trotting infantry kept pace beside each one, often hidden by fans of snow tossed into the air by the tracks and deep-treaded tyres as the vehicles turned.

The lieutenant's body lay close by. Andrea reached out and prised the frost-covered image intensifier from its grasp. 'This is hardly needed, they are not bothering to black-out.'

That fact was already apparent to Hyde, who was watching the activity around the door to the tower. 'No, they're acting as if they've got a right to be here. Either Sweden has gone over to their side, or it's had another bloody concession wrung out of it. Whichever it is, I still want to get these cruds back to the major, so curb that bloodlust of yours a bit longer.'

'Sarge, I been looking at those vehicles the Commies are bringing ashore.' Squeezing between the girl and NCO, Ripper nonchalantly leant against Andrea, until the blade of her shining bayonet gently rested on his arm and drew away to leave a neat-edged tear, several inches long. 'Looks to me like there ain't too much to be worried about. Apart from those two tanks, the only other wagons I can see with any sort of armament are those six-wheeled anti-aircraft rigs. Heck, they can't hurt us with those.'

'And what if Command send a chopper to pick us off this godforsaken lump of frozen rock when the excitement's over. You still think they'll be nothing to worry about then?'

'I hadn't thought about that.'

'Well try thinking before you decide to exercise your mouth the next time.' After the initial confusion and coming and going around the tower, Hyde hadn't been able to discern any special excitement among the Russians about the absence of the four agents he'd bagged, or the state of the wrecked room. Equipment was already being moved into it, and the debris-like possessions of the previous temporary occupants thrown out. That was like the Communists though, to cut their losses. The four Swedes obviously only constituted a sideshow of some sort; it was probably a relief to the commander on the spot not to have to deal with them.

There were no signs as yet that the Russians intended to start patrolling, at least none that Hyde could see. They appeared far more busy with the problems of erecting large radar dishes and antennae on the roofs of various vehicles, and guying tall sectional radio masts. Infantry, or they may have been armed engineers, were setting to work digging a seemingly haphazard scattering of slit- trenches, showing scant enthusiasm and making little progress.

'We'd better get going in case they start to spread out a bit.' As he began to get stiffly to his feet, Hyde heard the commotion behind him, and turned in time to see the young blond hurdle Hogg's corpse and start for the tower. A knife protruded from Dooley's shoulder and, even as he looked, Hyde heard the sharp snap of breaking bone as the big man forced back the bearded Swede's head to an impossible angle.

Andrea left her rifle in the snow. Before she was into her stride her hand had found and fastened on the knife tucked into her belt. It was the weapon Dooley had given her, and as she pulled it free and came up to her fleeing quarry his words were in her mind. His lessons guided her actions, and she didn't make the mistake of attempting to stab the running man; instead she went for a slashing cut that enabled her to keep her balance as she kept pace with her prey.

Seeing his pursuer from the corner of his eye, the blond half-turned and raised an arm to ward off the blow, red-tinged spittle flying from his damaged mouth as he made to form a shout. The heavy saw-backed blade sliced across his head and neck, from below his right ear to the top of his left shoulder. Blood and steam gushed into his collar as the tissue peeled apart, but he kept going, only now his steps were shorter, more deliberate, like an automaton.

Mouth still agape and spouting his life the Swede went down, toppling forward, not putting up a hand to fend off the impact the snow did little to soften. A geyser of blood and vapour stained his woollen hat and fair hair.

Jumping to land with both knees in the centre of her victim's back, Andrea clenched her hands about the sticky hilt of the knife and plunged it down into his back with all the force she could muster. On the second blow, the body gave a convulsive shudder that Andrea's slight weight couldn't subdue, and was finally still.

She did not dismount, remaining where she was until she once again had her breathing under control. Then, slowly and deliberately, she wiped the blade on the would-be escaper's clothing with long careful strokes. Crouched beside the body, she looked for any signs that the chase and kill might have been seen by anyone among the swarms of soldiers and technicians working within the distant oasis of artificial light. Satisfied, she began to drag the corpse back into the trees.

It was the first time she'd had occasion to use the knife, or put its ex-owner's instructions into practice. There was much else she had learnt, and even more still to absorb; she looked forward to applying all of it as effectively.

'Will you pull this bloody thing out!' Dooley indicated the hilt sticking from the front of his left shoulder. 'Every time I fucking move I feel the shitty point scraping on bone. It's making my teeth stand on edge. I'd rather drag my fingers down a blackboard.'

'Shouldn't have been so ruddy slow and given him the

chance to stick you.' Taking hold of the knife with his free hand, Hyde spread his fingers about the entry point to hold back the flesh as he withdrew it.

'I thought the fucker was half-dead. After the way he bounced off the door into the wall he should have been.' As the sergeant began to apply a steady pull, Dooley sought around for a topic to give himself a distraction from the increasing pain as the metal started to slide from his flesh. 'Could we move a few feet? The crud I snapped is beginning to stink. That's the bloody trouble with doing the job by hand, gives them time for a last shit when they realise what's happening.'

Having finished covering the blond with snow, Ripper commenced the same operation on the other body. The man's beard was tucked tightly over his left shoulder in an extreme contortion, livid marks banded his neck, and his tongue, swollen and purple, poked final derision at the life he had fled. Foul smells emanated from the stained and steaming clothing about the lower half of his body.

'Wait.' Pushing the American aside, Andrea wrenched at the Swede's clothing and tugged two belts from their loops.

'You taking trophies now?' Hyde watched without comment until she had finished and stood back.

'The woman,' Andrea indicated the glazed-eyed occupant of the sledge, now semi-conscious and moaning softly, and the bruised individual who had taken the brunt of Dooley's shoulder-charge, 'and that worm should be gagged.'

'And you'd just love to do it, wouldn't you?' Hyde snatched the twin strips of pliant leather. 'You know bloody well that if you half-block their mouths in these temperatures their spit will freeze and fill their throats and kill them. If they get stroppy we'll take care of it then, my way. Anyway, she's struggling for every breath, I can't see her starting to make a fuss. And the worm as you call him, well, take a look for yourself. Do you reckon he's about to do anything heroic?'

The surviving male of the party seemed to shrink at

Hyde's words, somehow collapsing in upon himself to occupy only half the space he had before. His face was a ghastly colour, it had passed white and was now a deep-lined grey. A palsied shaking gripped his body and he held both hands to his mouth, as though he would have bitten every nail simultaneously if he could have got them all in.

'That'll do, Ripper. I want them covered, not used to form the base for a new ice shield.' Shouldering his rifle, Hyde took up a trace from the sledge and forced it into the quaking Swede's hand, almost having to drag it from his mouth to do so. Ice crusted the exposed fingers before the Swede could pull his gloves on, and he whimpered at the pain of moving them. 'Right, if everybody is ready.' Holding another of the lines himself, Hyde took up the slack and prepared to pull.

'I were kinda thinking we ought to be making a move.' Alternately using borrowed binoculars and an image intensifier, Ripper had been maintaining surveillance of the Russian encampment. The three Gecko missile launchers had left the main body of the landing party and were motoring towards their cover. A command car, its canvas top erected and its windows thickly misted, headed the procession. 'They ain't coming on like they were looking for trouble, but if they intend to set up shop around here, then we are, if we don't get our tails out of here.'

Pushing back his hood, Dooley looked up at the tops of the trees. 'So do I, but I think we might have screwed the timing. Down!'

Faint at first, it grew rapidly louder, a buzzing whirring sound that raced up the audible range until it filled the air and assaulted their eardrums, almost drowning Dooley's shouted warning. Flying snow stung their faces, caked their clothes and plugged their nostrils. A helicopter's landing lights briefly seared night from the woods as it passed over, lighting the scattered bodies like day as Hyde's squad joined the corpses in the cover of the snow.

TEN

'Those Ruskies must be planning a long stay, that's a lot of equipment they're bringing ashore. There can't be much left in that transport by now, apart from the crew, fixtures and fittings.' Squinting at the surface radar screen, Cline watched the trace of a landing craft as it made another journey from the *Ivan Rogov's* flooded stern dock back to the north of the island.

The air-watch radar also showed activity. Five full loads of personnel and stores had already been ferried to the island by the big transport helicopter they had seen manhandled from the *Rogov's* battered hangar. It was approaching the ship again for another landing on the forward well-deck, where the TV display showed further crates and crowds awaiting it.

'Pity there isn't a nice thick minefield strung out across the island, between them and us.' York took his headphones off and rubbed his ears.

'Minefields are OK in some tactical situations, like protecting flanks, but not here.' There was a burning sensation at the back of Revell's eyes; he would have rubbed them but they were already sore. In a minute he'd go and get another scoop of ice to cool and soothe them. Sleep would have been better, but there wasn't the time for that luxury. 'No, if we set a few the Ruskies could either jump back into their boats and nip round them, or into that chopper and hop over. All we can do is hide, that's our only defence from what's piling up against us.'

'Another update coming in, Major.' York read the strip as it came out. 'The number of escorts is up to forty, heavies total fourteen. That looks like the final count.'

'That's enough. What's their ETA?' Revell had already computed his own estimate of the fleet's time of arrival, but with the benefit of near continual satellite surveillance, Command should be able to refine the probable error to within thirty minutes either way. Apart from anything else, it was better informed as to sea and ice conditions in the waters through which they must pass.

'Six hours, Major. That's two after first light.'

'You getting anything special, Boris?' The Russian had been so quiet that Revell had almost forgotten him. The man sat hunched at the side of the radio table, occasionally jotting a note down into his log, or attempting to adjust his ill-fitting headset.

'Nothing of significance, no. There is some ship-to-shore chatter, and the helicopter pilot keeps making complaints about the poor landing guidance he is getting on the *Rogov,* but that is all.'

'Well, stay on it. Let me know if they start moving about on the ground. Listen for anything about Hyde and the others.'

'They must be dead, or in the bag by now, Major.' Wiping his oil-streaked hands on his anorak, Libby came in from the kitchen. Burke could still be heard fussing and swearing over the erratically running generator.

'If they were,' Boris looked up, 'then these would be burning my ears.' He tapped the headphones. 'And we could expect visitors at any moment.'

'There's a chance we'll have some anyway, let's reduce the odds as much as we can. Close down every active system . . . yes, everything.' Revell waved his hand to quell the babble that greeted the order.

'Major, me and Burke have just spent half the night getting that bloody generator to go, and keeping it going.' Libby made the loudest protest. 'Now you want us to stop it?'

'That's right. We'll just keep a radio watch. That should

give us ample warning of increased activity by our Commie neighbours.' Even as he said it, Revell was all too well aware that it really didn't matter just how much warning they got of any Soviet aggression towards them. They didn't even have the men to provide an adequate defence of the house, let alone send reinforcements to aid the gunners at any of the three launch sites. The mission had been envisaged, by the most optimistic, as a hit and run affair: with their numbers so depleted, the very best that could be hoped for was hit and internment, and it was much more likely to be attempt-to-hit, and die. The continuing cold was making him feel ill, and lack of sleep didn't help. His every movement was becoming an effort. When your body hurt and ached all over, the temptation to do nothing, to just sit and wait for the end, was very great.

At this stage, inactivity might be a defence of sorts, but it offered no opportunity for rest. Perhaps some of the others might stand down for an hour at a time, but he couldn't. Eventually it would get to him, perhaps not on this operation; but if he went on to more, then one day he would find his mind had a limit to what it could take. Every combat officer had a breaking point, a moment at which the strain or tension would become too much and his brain would simply switch off. Many others had gone that way before him. He'd seen some – who had refused to give in to increasingly obvious symptoms of an approaching nervous collapse until it was too late – go to pieces. A colonel who had burst into tears when only a dozen men out of a fresh battalion had rallied after a massed Russian attack, a young lieutenant who had beaten out the last flames on the shrivelled pain-wracked bodies of his baled-out crew and then calmly walked back to his blazing tank and climbed in a moment before its ammo detonated . . . so many different ways to go when a mind overruled the will that had been driving it too long, and tried to regain control. He was already watching himself for the first signs, watching and waiting.

There was the sound of heavy, hesitant, footsteps on

the stairs, a drumming double thump kept time. The medic appeared, dragging the body of a gunner.

'Give him a hand, Clarence.' A moment passed before Revell realised the sniper had made no move to leave the dark corner where he sat. 'I said help him.'

With slow deliberation, Clarence stood up still kneading his fingers, as he had been doing perpetually since the moment he'd recovered his senses after his brush with freezing death. Without the light from the tubes he couldn't examine them to see if the faint discolouration had gone, but the tips didn't hurt any more. 'You want me to help carry a body?'

'That's it, got it in one. And why not? That poor guy would be happy to cart you, all around the island I should imagine, if that was the price of reversing your positions. Don't make a fuss, just do it.'

Teeth clenched, an expression of extreme distaste on his face, Clarence took hold of the body by the ankles and helped carry it out. It joined a row of six others beside the wall of the house.

'Two more will join them soon.' Private Fraser stared at the line. 'Nothing I can do for them you see. Don't matter what I cover them with, they can't move about, the cold just creeps into them and they slip away.'

'I know what it's like.' Clarence continually wiped his hands down his side to brush away the thought of the contact he'd just had to endure. He hated the feel of another person close to him, and physical contact forced him to fight the urge to lash out and end it, before he was sick. Handling the body, even though he'd only been touching the corpse's stiffened boots, had been as repugnant to him as enduring the jostling proximity of a crowd. He knew the feeling was an abnormal one, but had long since ceased to try to curb or cure it. Somehow it was as if the manner in which he had cut himself off from all emotional contact with others had not been enough. 'Let's get back inside before we stay out here with him permanently.'

The silence and near total darkness inside the house

110

were oppressive, but that suited Clarence. Even the cold, after what it had almost done to him, seemed on his side; forcing each man to withdraw within whatever lagging-like bundle of rags and dead man's clothes he could gather and hold about him. Feeling his way along the wall back to his place, Clarence squatted and picked up his Enfield. Even the sacking bindings could not hide its familiar detail from him. As though it were an extension of himself, the forged and machined metal slipped comfortably into his grasp. He held it close, bowing forward until he rested his forehead against the jute-draped barrel. Reaching out, he patted his pack and then pulled it closer. Not that there had ever been any danger of it being taken. He would find a use for those special rounds, he was sure of that, absolutely sure. The feeling was one he'd had before, and it had never been wrong yet.

In the pitch-black of the interior Revell was also alone. Command did that for a man, and he did nothing to lessen it. Responsibility had brought him remoteness, as well as respect and obedience. But it wasn't just the rank: example and tough discipline had been the most important contributory factors. Other officers were able to combine that with an ability to mix, even to be familiar, with the men: but of his own choice Revell didn't, or maybe it was nearer the truth to say he couldn't. That was a hard thing to admit to himself. He'd not formed a stable relationship of any kind, not since his divorce. In a way, it was as if he didn't trust people any more. It was OK to work with them, or in the case of his women, have a brief affair with them, but never anything closer. And here, in the Zone, getting to know someone well could be a mistake. The Zone had a way of ruthlessly breaking up partnerships, friendships . . . permanently.

'I wonder where Hyde is now, and the lieutenant . . .'

'And the girl.' It was York who tacked on an end to Libby's sentence.

'Who knows.' Burke's voice floated in from the kitchen, where he was curled up against the warm metal of the generator. 'All I know is that wherever I was with her, I could keep warm.'

111

Revell almost snapped a slap-down, to put an end to the exchange, but administered one to himself instead, and said nothing. He let the conversation flow on, only half-heard it as it degenerated into an obscene version of tennis, with the men's dirty minds providing the rackets, and their speculations about Andrea, the balls. Upstairs he could hear Fraser moving about. The medic was having a tough time. All he could do was watch his patients die, and he was taking it hard. But at least he had that to keep him occupied. For the rest of them, there were hours to be passed in which there would be nothing to do but sit, or pace, and wait. Anything that prompted them to action before the ships came into range would be bad news, unless it was Hyde returning; and as the minutes ticked by, and the temperature continued to drop, the chances of that became more and more remote

'. . .and if I know the sarge,' Burke was having the last say, concluding with a tone of authoritive finality, 'he'll have found somewhere nice and snug, and he'll be waiting for the Ruskies to settle down before trekking back. I bet you, nice and snug . . .'

'Frostbite.' Fraser cut away the woman's boot, rolled down her thick socks and pulled them off. To mid-calf, her leg was an ugly purplish-black. 'That's worse than anything I've ever seen.' He tentatively touched the hardend skin. It was rough and cracked, like ill-kept parchment. 'Come to that, it's worse than anything I've ever heard of.'

'Heck, it was hard enough keeping the rest of us from going that way, we couldn't look after that Commie dame as well.' Ripper was bent over, his arms crossed and his hands beneath his armpits, nursing feeling back into his limbs and fighting the pain as circulation gradually returned.

'What about him?' Hyde toed the Swede on the floor. The man was breathing badly, his chest heaving at each laboured breath, every exertion making his eyes roll to leave only the whites showing.

'Looks like a heart attack. I haven't got the time for him.' With those words Fraser dismissed the dying man and went on attending to the woman. 'Back at base hospital it was the MOs who had all the cases like that, all I did was splinters in the bum and routine pox treatment . . .'

'Now he fucking tells us.'

The medic went on, ignoring Burke's interruption. '. . . but that's the way my uncle went. Nothing we can do for him.'

Using his elbow Burke gave Dooley's ribs a hefty double-nudge. 'Must've been the big cuddle-up with our German piece that made his ticker give out. A few hours close with her and I reckon mine would overheat as well.'

'Fuck off.' For once Dooley made the effort and kept his hair-trigger temper in check. 'We kept together to keep warm, no one touched her, no one.' If Revell had not been near by, he might have, he *would* have smashed their driver in the face, driven his nose out through the back of his head. OK, so maybe he hadn't done all the things with her he'd boasted of to the others in the past, but she was still with him, and though from necessity Hyde and Ripper and the old Swede might have joined in the penguin-like huddle to stay warm, no one had touched her. No one would while he was around.

For Andrea, the Swede's collapse at the moment they reached the house had been a final irony. At every step the presence of the two Soviet agents had endangered them all. By increasing the size of the group they had made concealment more difficult, and in addition to slowing their return to a snail's crawl, the sledge had forced them to wait for first light so that they had a chance of picking a manageable route. And now as events had turned out they could have, they might as well have, left them behind. There would be nothing gleaned from either.

'Look's like the fickle finger of fate has done gone and saved you the worry of playing executioner.' Ice crusted Ripper's face, and flaked away as he grinned at Andrea

8   113

'Kinda seems a shame when I bet you got yourself all keyed up for it. Maybe the major will let you play with the bodies while they're still warm.'

· 'If he does, she can have this old Commie anytime.' Clumsily using his mittened hand, Libby closed the Swede's eyes. 'Looks like he might have been a school teacher.' He examined the dead man's palms. 'Doesn't seem to have done much real work.'

As the hand was released and flopped back to the floor, Andrea stepped on it, and twisted her boot to grind it until the bones began to crack. 'It is more likely he was from a university. In Sweden, as in most so-called free countries, they are breeding grounds for his type. Strange that men of such intelligence should be so naive, so pathetic as to believe the lies they are fed. He in his turn would have become a recruiter, taking his cue from his KGB control as to which people to ask to his parties, how to slant any article or paper he might write, and how, when there was an important pro-East or pro-West decision pending, to help the men in power reach the conclusion that Moscow wanted. He is the sort whose whispers, whose carefully phrased suggestions, would make an official think he was learning what the people wanted. The people . . . worms, to be shovelled first in one direction, then in another, or crushed, or buried.'

'There's shit like them in every country. Sweden doesn't have a monopoly.' Hyde indicated to Libby and Ripper to remove the body. The hatred that poured from her never ceased to surprise him. All of them loathed the Communists, he had more reason than most to feel that way, but with Andrea it was an obsession. And yet when they'd first found her she'd been with a gang of Grepo deserters, ex-East German border guards, scum, the lowest of the low. Hatred she might have in her, but to survive she was capable of tempering it: even better than Clarence, in whom no compromise was possible. A savage, brutal killer with a high degree of base animal cunning, that was how Hyde saw her. And yet her face was incredible, the features such that a man who appreciated beauty for its

114

own sake could look at it for hours. Hyde was well aware that looking was as close as he would ever get. It was probably as close as any of them would get, but while the others could entertain hopes, he couldn't. Not with his appearance, not ever . . .

Revell checked his watch. It was time to start living dangerously once more, really dangerously. Since the Ruskies had landed, there had been little chance of their being detected unless the enemy took the unlikely step of patrolling the whole island, but now they had to switch in all the systems again, and any detectors pointed their way, even by chance, would immediately pick up the emissions of their active radars. 'Let's have the generator going again. I want all systems functioning the moment the damned thing settles to a reasonably steady beat. Then get on to the gunners at the launch sites. I want status reports.

The silky material of the dead Swede's outer garments was making him difficult to lift, and the pair assigned to remove him had resorted to taking hold of a foot each, and dragging him unceremoniously. There was a dull thudding crack as the corpse's head bumped over and down the step. Jolted open by the rough passage, the man's locked stare contemplated the lightening sky. Walking to the door, Revell watched him being placed with the others.

He would have almost certainly have succumbed to the weather, even without their intervention. The old Commie had probably waited most of his adult life for this day, when Soviet troops would set foot on Swedish soil. All that time the traitor had plotted and schemed and waited, and when the moment had finally arrived and he'd been here ready to see it, Hyde and his section had spoilt it for him. No wonder his heart had given out. For a while, as he travelled to the island and began to get ready, he must have believed that this was the dawning of his ambitions. He must have held the conviction that the limited landing was simply a first step that would eventually lead to Sweden falling into the Soviet net, and his assumption of some position of puppet power. Now there would be none of that. His body, stiffening but still showing a degree of elasticity, struck the frozen form of a gunner, and flopped off to sprawl untidily in the snow.

Ripper paused before going back in, screwing up his face as he examined the unnatural colour of the sky. The dawn had been tinged a distinctive red, but now it was rapidly whitening. Ice formed on the rims of his nostrils and around his mouth as he peered at the phenomenon. 'That's kinda pretty. I ain't never seen a sky that colour.'

'Most people who see it never see anything else ever again.' Standing behind Revell, Boris had also seen the effect. 'The red you saw first light was caused by all the dust and contamination in the air, that is nothing; what you see now though has been given many names, usually it is called diamond dust. Look at your sleeves, move them.'

'Hey, I'm going solid,' Not knowing what to expect, what to look for, Ripper flexed his arm. A white crust had formed on the surface, and as the coated material reluctantly creased, splits appeared in it. 'Will you look at that, it's like the damned stuff had been dipped in dry ice.'

'My country sees the most severe of weather, but even there such a thing is a rarity.' Boris moved aside to let the men in. 'It only happens when the temperature drops below minus sixty. Ice particles form on the dust, they settle and cover everything they touch with a mantle of white death. In minutes a man can suffocate, even faster than the lieutenant did, as thicker and thicker deposits build up around the mouth. So it would seem we now face a new enemy.'

'We've been facing that enemy since we landed.' Carefully, but still painfully, Revell chipped, prised and peeled the frozen crust from his mouth. 'Just seems like Jack Frost is getting reinforcements.'

In the kitchen the generator fired at Burke's first attempt, making an infernal racket until the covers were hastily replaced and it warmed to run at a steady pace that reduced vibration.

'Everybody to stations. Sergeant Hyde, I want anyone who doesn't have a specific task to be armed and ready to move at a moment's notice. The intruder alarms don't allow much of a margin, so you'll have to be prepared to respond to any incursion immediately.'

'We'll be ready, Major, not many of us, and not with much, but we'll be ready.' There was no need for Hyde to pass on the instruction, the others had heard and were already checking weapons and ammunition. Except for Burke. Hyde watched the man as he pretended to busy himself with a minor detail about the generator. 'You've never been keen to do a job in your whole life, Burke, you're not conning me. That mechanical marvel sounds fair enough, put your gear together and join us in here where I can keep an eye on you.'

'Isn't it good.' Burke saw the sergeant watching him from the doorway. 'For a bloody year you've been on at me to do this, that and the other, and now just as I get me teeth into a job you want me to drop it and go play bleeding Cowboys and Indians again.' He went to wipe the grease from his hands, then decided against it, leaving on the protective layer and pulling his mittens over his still slippery palms. 'A ruddy combat driver I'm supposed to be, a bloke who pilots battle-taxis. Alright, so I've been a silly sod and made a cross for me own back by taking on every piddling job that's had anything to do with mechanics, but why the hell are you always roping me in to do the do-and-die bit?'

'I don't always need a reason, but this time it's because we need manpower, and even you might be some use.'

'As a human shield, maybe.' Making no attempt to conceal his amusement, Dooley poked their driver with the snout of a light machine gun. 'Anyway, don't worry, little man, you can just stand around trying to look ferocious until the action starts, and that won't be for ages yet.'

'You're wrong.' The instant the surface radar screen glowed into life, Cline spotted the distinct traces. He began to count. 'There's five, six, no, seven,' he added the correction as yet another blip materialised, 'seven ships coming out of the Sound.'

The men crowded behind him for a look, as an eight then a ninth appeared. It was Dooley who broke what seemed like a long silence.

'Jesus Christ. The bastards are rushing us.'

ELEVEN

'Looks like two cruisers and an escort group, destroyers most likely.'

The radar man's interpretation of the contacts struck Revell as about right. He'd been expecting a vanguard of approximately that strength. 'Good, now check the sites, find out what sort of shape your gunners are in.'

As he waited for the information, Revell unwrapped and made a quick visual inspection of his 12-gauge assault rifle. He'd debated with himself whether or not to bring it on this mission. Useful as a close-quarters weapon, he was now beginning to think he might have done better to bring something with a longer range, especially in view of their shortage of fire power, and medium and heavy support weapons.

'Two of the men at the Lance site have collapsed, Major. Sounds like exposure. Everyone else is ready to go.'

Damn the bombardier, Revell disliked the way the man always had to have an opinion on every matter. If York was the man who thought he could do it all, Cline was the individual who imagined he knew it all. 'OK, tell site three they'll have to look after them the best they can for the time being.'

'At least the manpower shortage won't matter so much there.' Hyde was removing some of the ammunition belts with which Dooley had festooned himself. 'It's one and two that'll need the fit men for reloading.' He left four of the hundred-round belts on the big man, and handed him the others to be replaced in the ammunition boxes.

'Yeah, chucking those fucking great rockets around they'll be collapsing from exhaustion. Wouldn't happen if everyone was as fit as me.'

'Oh shut up, Dooley.' There was a note of irritation in Libby's voice. 'First you show off by loading yourself until you look like an ammo tech's Christmas tree, then you go for a new hot air production record. You're not going to tell us about the time you did five hundred press-ups to get your Kung-Fu black belt, are you? Not again.'

'Keep your men quiet, Sergeant.'

The officer's words having been audible to everyone in the room, Hyde didn't need to repeat them, but he added a rider of his own. 'Some of you lot have been treating this like a bloody picnic so far; wise up, or you'll find you've got an enemy facing you already. Now settle down.'

In the ensuing silence, the only sound was that coming from the generator. Scuffling movement upstairs announced the commencement of another. Hesitant heavy footsteps on the stairs preceded the noise of a body being dragged down them.

'Picnic's over for another bloke.' Scrutinising the floor, Burke hoped he wouldn't be detected. His view was suddenly blocked by Hyde's boots, but to his amazement nothing was said, and the boots moved out of his range of vision. That wasn't like the sarge at all, not at all. The scar-faced bugger had never soft pedalled before, probably didn't know how to. He risked a glance. Their senior NCO had crossed to the radar screen.

Knowing Burke would be watching, Hyde turned slowly and the knife-slash gash of a mouth below where his nose should have been widened a fraction. It was the nearest he could get to a grin. 'Could be cancelled for all of us. Six more major units are coming out of the Sound, with enough escorts to make ruddy great stepping stones all the way over to Denmark. You want to stay alive, you'd better put in the maximum effort the major will be expecting of everybody else. For the time being that just means staying awake and staying alert, that should break you into the idea nice and gently.'

Cline's application to his task was already total. At present his concentration was focused on the surface radar. The air-watch and perimeter intruder systems were switched to automatic, an audible warning would sound if either detected interlopers. In the case of the air-watch radar there was a further refinement. At the instant of contact the set would interrogate any aircraft with its IFF. Should the Identification-Friend-or-Foe fail to receive the correct answer, then the alarm it blared out would rise to a more strident note that no one could miss. There was no need, while the system continuously monitored and checked its own performance and its tiny green tell-tale glowed, for Cline to do so; but exhibiting religious dedication, Cline double-checked it every couple of minutes anyway.

He did it ostentatiously, moving his whole head, not merely glancing up but taking a long hard look. By the book, that was how he intended to do it. His backside ached, as did the back of his thighs,; the fronts of his legs, and his feet and arms were cold. The numbing chill had crept into his body and even now he could feel it spreading through him. He had tightened-up. To the very last atom of his bones and flesh. Shoulders hunched, stomach drawn in, a feeling of tense, almost painful constriction had invaded him.

'Try one of these.'

An unthinking refusal of the grubby mint Ripper was offering was stifled by Cline before it could be expressed. 'Are they hot?'

'Only about the hottest thing around here, apart from Andrea that is.'

The off-white disc seared Cline's tongue on contact, then branded the inside of his cheek as he pushed it aside to suck in cold air.

Ripper watched the radio-man's reaction, saw the beads of sweat that broke out on his forehead. 'You like it, heh? I sure do.' He popped two into his mouth and chewed hard. 'Really do warm you, don't they? I used to eat a packet before going home of a night, so my mom wouldn't know I'd been having a beer or two. Kinda got a liking for them. Want another?'

As Cline shunted the caustic sweet around his mouth, he became aware of the others watching him. Well he wasn't about to give them any satisfaction. Taking a deep breath, he gathered all the saliva he could and swallowed. Every inch of the confection's route down his throat to his stomach was charted by a burning sensation. He could feel a small ball of fire where it finally came to rest in his belly. 'I'll have another.'

'You haven't the time. Keep your attention on the screen.'

The officer's intervention came just in time, for the packet was being extended towards the bombardier again. Cline was relieved, he hadn't been too confident of his ability to palm a mint without being observed.

Having finished his checks of the men and their weapons, Hyde picked a corner of the room and settled down. Within an hour, two at the most, they'd all know whether or not they'd be coming through the mission, and if so in what condition. His small squad were less occupied than York or Cline or the major. Even their Russian had something to do, but for those of them who hadn't, now was the time to be thinking about all the things that had already gone wrong, and what could still do so.

It was Ripper who showed the pressure most. He had the least combat experience of any of them and was conscious of the fact. Like with the practical joke he'd played on the bombardier, he was overcompensating in an attempt to conceal his fear. All of the others had been through it many times before, only Dooley displayed any nervousness, but then he always did. He reminded Hyde of a big bull, pawing the ground, almost too eager for the action to commence. 'Where the hell are you going?'

'I never searched that old guy we chucked outside.' Dooley halted at the door.

'The major checked him for papers.'

'That ain't what I mean, Sarge . . . Jesus, do I have to spell it out? Look, the old goat must have had some money on him. If we end up getting interned, might be useful to have a few krona stashed away.'

'Don't try lying to me, Dooley, you're just no good at it. Why do you think you always lose at cards?'

'Honest, Sarge . . .'

'Honest my arse.' Hyde raised his voice. 'Sit down. I know what you're up to. Ever since Cohen got in the way of that tank shell at Frankfurt you've been trying to copy him, build a little fortune for yourself. Forget it, you haven't the wits to amass it or the brains to hold on to it, so quit trying. Anyway, if we get grabbed by the Swedes, what do you imagine they'll think if they find we've been killing and looting the bodies of their nationals. Leave that frozen carcase alone, find something else to occupy your time.'

'I don't see the harm in trying to come out of the war with a bit more to show for it than a load of scars.' Grumbling in an undertone, Dooley sat down beside Andrea. She went on polishing her bayonet, appearing not to hear him, so he persisted in nudging her until he had her reluctant attention. 'Well, what do you think? You remember Cohen, the little runty Yid who had the pockets of his flak-jacket stuffed with money and rings. Why shouldn't I do that?'

'If you wish to, you can.' Andrea folded the soft pink cloth and tucked it into a pocket. 'There are fortunes to be made in a war. Even in the camps there are refugees who have done well out of the suffering of others. Many Russian soldiers have also profited. When I was with the GDR people's militia, many times I had to help load trains and convoys of trucks with goods the Soviets were stealing from my people. So if you wish, then gather what money you can, but while you do it remember all those you have seen die because their need, or their greed, made them reach too far, just once too often.'

'What a nice little moral tale.' Sitting on the other side of the girl, Libby couldn't resist the sneer. 'Since when have you been writing sermons? I thought all your energies were devoted to learning new ways to kill.'

'Piss off, this is a private conversation.' Dooley could feel tension growing like a physical thing inside him.

Clarence knew what she meant, understood the point she was trying to make. It was stupid, he'd only started to understand her since she had deserted him in favour of Dooley. There was something deep inside Andrea that drove her on. Her fanatical hatred of the Communists was real enough, but that was only a surface manifestation of what lay beneath. With her brains she could have got out of the Zone, or at least used her looks to better her situation, but she had chosen to stay among the people at the bottom of the heap. Even now she operated with this ragbag unit when she could have found something much better. It was as if she needed it to be that way, needed to see and experience the suffering. And what she saw at first-hand fed her hatred and helped her kill and, coming full circle, the killing then compounded the horrors she'd witnessed. A fruitless cycle of death, whose beginning was unknown and whose inevitable end, after many, many turns, must be violent and bloody.

'Those Ruskie sailors aren't the best at station keeping, Major.' Cline had to revise his log entries as the enemy ships veered from heading to heading. 'If I allow for the wandering about, take a sort of average course, then it looks like they'll pass within three miles of the island. We'll be able to take them on at point-blank range. You want me to alert the launcher crews?'

'We're not engaging the vanguard.' Revell saw the look Cline gave him, and was tantalisingly slow in adding, 'Not yet. Once those Ruskies figure out what's coming at them, and from where, our target practise will be over. I want to engage the maximum number of targets in the shortest possible time. Let the lead group pass, we'll give the cruisers a few rounds from astern, but save most of the rounds for the next bunch. We might not get the chance to use our reloads. I want to do all the damage we can with what rockets are in the tubes now.'

'What about the *Ivan Rogov*? That damned tub is sitting in our laps.' York had turned to an illustration of a sister ship. 'That baby packs a hell of a punch. Says here she's got guns and missiles of her own. If her captain decided to join the fight, we're a sitting target.'

'So is he.' The cold must be more than numbing his body. That was something Revell should have thought of for himself. What else had he missed, what else was there that he was overlooking? For many hours now the *Rogov* had been a part of the local scene, he'd grown used to its presence until it had merged into the background and he'd come close to forgetting, damn it, he *had* forgotten it. 'If it'll put your mind at ease, York, then we'll give the tub the undivided attention of half a dozen rounds, how does that suit you?'

'Just fine, Major. Want me to let you know of anything else I think of?'

'I believe you may be, as you Americans say, pushing your luck.' Boris rapped the radio-man's ankle with the steel-shod side of his boot. He said the words quietly enough not to carry to the officer, but still managed to inject the urgent note of warning he intended.

'Vanguard is coming into camera range now.'

Under Cline's practised guidance a TV camera panned over an expanse of slab-dotted sea. He switched to a second, and instantly the screen was filled with a bow-on shot of an ice-coated destroyer. An arcing bow wave carried a crescent of ice and foam up and away from the knife-edged hull.

'Pennant number is five-six-four.' Having retrieved his book, Cline sought the vessel's identity. 'Here it is, *Strogiy*, modified Kashin class destroyer. Last reported in Leningrad yards for extensive refit.'

'Find and identify the others, especially the two cruis-ers.'

Revell stood away from the bombardier's chair. The operator would be under sufficient pressure without his appearing to hover over him. One after another the vanguard escorts jumped into focus, were identified and logged. In several cases the ships could only be identified by class or type, their pennant numbers were as new as the hulls, and unlisted. A guided missile frigate was of a class never seen before, and defied Cline's efforts to positively identify it.

'There's one of them.' A Kresta class cruiser jumped into vision. Going for a close-up, Cline panned along its impressive length. The ship bristled with a staggering array of antenna complexes and weaponry. A moment later he found a second, and this one he was able to identify. 'It's the *Marshal Voroshilov*, another that was last seen in the yards.'

'That's an anti-submarine force. Our subs are going to have a tough time with that crowd.' Revell scanned the list.

'If we used all the tubes, we could do them a fair bit of damage, give our blokes a chance.' Only two buttons had to be depressed and Cline could immediately transmit the ships' positions to the launcher crews. He'd been with the battery long enough to know that it would take the gunners mere seconds to align the tubes and get clear. In a matter of minutes the Russian ships would be on the receiving end of a storm of fragmentation warheads that would rip through their complex radar equipment and mow down any crew on deck or behind light protection.

'No, they'll have to take care of themselves. Our orders say we go for the big tubs.' On the screen the view of the ships was changing from side-on to a three-quarter rear shot. 'Have number one site prepare to engage the cruisers. Seven rounds each. Site two can put a half dozen rounds into the *Rogov*.' Revell turned to York. 'And this is where you start to do your work. The moment we open fire, start playing with your fireworks. I want any Commie tracker who so much as glances this way to get thoroughly confused. Use chaff, ECM, whatever you need to decoy any radar homing warheads they throw, but go easy on the pyrotechnics. Libby salvaged what he could, but we're still short, so make it last, be sparing. I want maximum value from what we've got.'

With his headphones on, Boris could only half-hear what was going on, he would have preferred not to have been able to hear at all. When he had been drafted into the Russian forces, especially when he took the military oath, the penalties for desertion had been drummed into him. They were harsh, and usually demanded the ultimate sanction, but he was discovering that there were other penalties that no one had warned him about.

To fight Communism was one thing, but when he had actually made the decision to join the NATO army he had not given much thought to just what that might, that would, that was about to, involve. He had friends, some of whom had been drafted at the same time, others he had made during training or in his unit, and now he was about to help in the destruction of fellow Russians, men he might have got to know and like in other circumstances. The Soviet navy got the pick of the best electronics experts; perhaps some of his friends were aboard those ships, it was possible, likely even. The only difference between him and them was that he'd had his chance to escape, and had taken it. But then he'd been free to, with no close family ties . . . free; free to turn round and kill his own people. Some of whom he could hear talking at that very moment.

It sounded like ship-to-shore transmissions again, nothing important, just a junior sergeant complaining about a mistake over rations that had come ashore; he was telling the ship that they had no tea or vodka and that his officers expected him to remedy the situation. From the other end, and a bored supply clerk on the *Rogov* was verbally shrugging aside the complaint; he was safe and had no wish to bring the mistake to the notice of his own superiors.

Perhaps the clerk had done it deliberately, to pocket the profit he would make from selling the precious supplies elsewhere. Everyone did it, or tried to. It was necessary if a man were to survive in the Russian forces. A case of vodka supplied to an officer at a special low price would build up a fund of, if not goodwill, at least understanding, that might come in very useful later on. Boris caught the start of another exchange between Cline and the officer, and closed his ears to it. There was no way he could entirely disassociate himself from what was about to happen, but he was determined to have as little to do with it as possible. That would not salve his conscience, but if he did not know everything that happened, at least he would carry a smaller burden.

'You still want to hit those cruisers, Major?'

As the radar screen showed the vanguard moving away from the island still heading due north, the second and much larger group was moving into range of their TV cameras. Abandoning close-ups, Cline had gone for a panoramic view. To the limit of the depth of the field, the floe-sprinkled sea was filled with wave throwing, rime-coated warships from dashing frigates of three thousand tons, to a towering Archangel class cruiser of sixteen thousand tons. Missiles and high-angle guns pointed skyward on every one, while their assorted radars rotated in endless search of the sky and sea.

'I can't get them all on to the screen at once, I've got a swarm of traces on the radar, how do I choose targets?'

'Pick the biggest. Leningrad can churn out frigates and destroyers like mincemeat, cruisers take longer, cost a lot more. Don't try skimping, better to send ten rockets at one target so that a couple get through, than send two at each of five targets and have them all hacked down before they get within lethal range.'

'You hear that?' Libby snorted. 'Lethal my fucking foot. It'll be like trying to total a wasp's nest by punching it.'

'I found you need a good sense of the fucking ridiculous in this outfit. Look at us.' Despite his words, Dooley did not stand up and offer himself for inspection. 'There's Cline and the major getting ready to have a go at better than a hundred thousand tons of armoured shipping with maybe a ton or two of fragmentation warheads, and us, sitting here with shitty rifles and machine guns, waiting to take on a battalion of Soviet marines. Now if that ain't fucking silly, what is? After I got in a couple of fights with guys who called me a liar when I tried telling them about some of the missions we've been on, I gave up. It gets you down, don't it?'

'It do, it sure do.' Ripper nodded sagely, until Dooley rapped him hard on the head and rammed his helmet down over his eyes.

Revell tapped Cline on the shoulder when the last of the target co-ordinates were punched in. The ringing clang made by Dooley's fist on the shaped steel dome died away as Revell leant forward and spoke quietly to the bombardier.

'Open fire.'

TWELVE

Both launchers were fired at the same instant, but it was the rockets sent against the anchored amphibious warfare ship that found their mark first.

Caught off-guard by an attack from a totally unexpected direction, the ship's radar-directed gatlings didn't even open fire, and every warhead got through.

Two exploded over the bridge, sending a storm of white-hot fragments into the unarmoured upperworks and totally destroying the vessel's fit of radar masts and dishes. As the remains of the tall lattice structure toppled on to the rear landing pad, the third warhead blasted the forward hanger and smashed a helicopter standing in front of it. Fire broke out immediately as aviation fuel spread in a blazing tide through the open doors and down into the bowels of the ship. The points of detonation of the last three rockets were lost amid the smoke and flying debris from the first, but the fact that they too had found their target could not be doubted when a huge bubble of flame rose from the ship's bow, as ready-use ammunition for the forward twin 76mm gun was ignited.

The rockets chasing the cruisers had further to travel, and two of those aimed at the lead ship did not reach it. Intercepted by streams of fire from the ship's gatlings, they were broken apart by the torrent of 23mm shells.

Against the warship's armour, the rockets' effects were not so spectacular, but as the smoke drifted clear one of the cruisers could be seen making a hard turn away to port, its antenna badly mauled and its helicopter pad, hanger and rear superstructure heavily scarred, with the barely recognisable wreckage of the chopper hanging over the ship's stern.

As the launchers rippled their heavy projectiles towards the ships, York activated the decoys. Small mortars hurled chaff high into the air over the island and a silver rain began to fall that would hopefully confuse enemy radars attempting to track the rockets' path back to their launch sites. Other shells landed well away from the house and began to transmit powerful signals that, for a short while, would dwarf the real emissions, and draw-off enemy warheads homing in on such sources.

While others might be able to watch the effects of the strike on metal, Boris could hear its effects on men. The weary supply clerk aboard the *Rogov* was drowned out for a moment as the salvo struck, then he could be heard shouting, then screaming. Boris could make out the words 'fire' and 'door', and finally after more frantic screaming, over and over again the one word 'mother'. It cut altogether as he reached for the tuner to shut off the sounds.

They'd done it, they'd got in the first blow. Plugging in a spare headset, Revell waited impatiently for the message that the launchers had been realigned on their fresh targets. Come on, come on. On his watch the seconds flickered by insanely fast. Site one was first, and two signalled ready an instant later. A glance at the screen told him there was no need for him to alter the targets chosen. As he gave the order, he imagined the launchers out there in the snow – only much of it would have melted around them by now. What was left would be blasted away by the back-wash as the remaining twenty-six rockets at one site, and thirty-four at the other, took off and rode their flame- tails towards the second group of ships.

This time the Russian vessels were ready. Cones of concentrated small-calibre fire reached out to the warheads aiming mindlessly for them, but some were getting through. The big anti-aircraft cruiser was surrounded by metal-lashed water as slivers of steel swept it and the sea about it.

The proximity fuse failed on one rocket and it impacted just forward of the bridge on another large warship. Tearing apart a pair of ready-to-fire surface-to-air missiles, it added the fuel of their spilled propellant and broken explosive content to the blaze that engulfed that section of the deck.

And of the many rockets that failed to get through, not every one was wasted. Two that failed to reach their target erupted in balls of flame above a dashing Grisha class corvette. It came out of the far side of the man-made storm with every plate pierced, heeling hard over in a tight uncontrolled turn that took it right under the bows of a destroyer, missing a collision by inches.

'All bloody hell has let loose.' As York sent the second set of decoys soaring high over the house, he turned to help Boris find the Russian wavelengths. 'Every damned position on the dial is in use, they don't know what the heck is going on.'

'The commander of the marines on the island is broadcasting to anyone who will listen that he is not leading a mutiny, he is telling the ships he has not opened fire. I think he is crying.'

'Let's hope the ships hit him instead of us. How's that re-loading going?'

'Give them time, Major. Forty tubes is a lot of metal to lift. Best possible is ten minutes, and that's pushing it.' Despite the spectacular things to be seen on the TV, it was the surface radar that presented Cline with the most interesting picture at the moment.

The first group of ships were still moving north, but at reduced speed. Now it was down from their previous thirty knots to less than twenty. But it was the traces showing the positions of the ships in the second group that were the most fascinating.

'They're all over the place. Look at them.' Revell put his finger on the screen to underline the two blips that were fast converging on a collision course. Disappointingly, they noticed their danger, but must still have suffered damage in the heavy side-swipe that seemed inevitable, judging by the temporary joining of the blobs of telltale light.

From somewhere out to sea came a series of dull explosions. A heavy movement of air shook the house and threw snow into the room through every gap and crack about the windows and doors.

'That's the *Rogov*. Those shits out there have got problems.' Unable to resist the temptation any longer, Dooley had come over to the radar desk and was trying to look between Revell and the operator to see what was happening on the screen.

Internal explosions were racking the ship, sending chunks of debris into the sea. Members of the crew lined the rail surrounding the aft helicopter pad, and at each fresh blast another would jump. Flames licked from every port and opening and sent a pillar of jet-black smoke straight up into the milky white of the sky. From its stern came a slab-fronted landing craft. The fact that it was already packed with men did not stop those at the rail from hurling themselves over the side to land in it. Several missed, and spun for a moment in the LCT's wake before going under the breath-stopping freezing water of the Kattegat.

Three ships among the second group appeared dead in the water. They were being left behind by the remainder as they moved on, with no vestige of formation remaining. Now, like a herd of cattle that had been frightened into a stampede, they were only interested in leaving the area as quickly as possible.

'Looks like we're going to get away with it.' Cline was filling pages of the log with cryptic notes in a hand that grew more extravagant in its flourishes with each entry. 'We beat a whole fleet to a pulp and we're being let off scot-free.'

'It's rather early to start counting chickens. There's still too many damned foxes around, others are finding that as well.' Using the radar, Revell had been following the progress of the LCT that had left the *Rogov*. As though its helmsman was undecided on the best course of action and the safest place of refuge, it had first circled out to sea, and now it turned back towards the island and crossed the path of the second group. Its charmed life came to an end as it crossed close in front of a large trace and abruptly disappeared.

'That must be the last of them coming now.' With the tip of his pencil Cline indicated the fresh traces springing to life at the base of the screen. A red light flashed urgently among an unlit row. 'Intruder, Major. Northern perimeter.'

'Any idea who or what or how many?'

'Can't be sure, Major. The equipment I brought was chosen more for lightness and compactness than multi-sensor capability, so I can't say if it was metal, or what, but it did last several seconds, so it could either be a slow-moving vehicle or a file of men.'

'That's nice.' Dooley and the rest of Hyde's group were getting ready to move. 'He don't know what it is, but it's either a tank or a war party.'

'What's the difference, we've got to stop it anyway.' Five grenades were already hanging from Libby's webbing, he added another two.

Hyde opened the door, and the temperature in the room dropped several degrees as soft milky light flooded in. 'So let's go and do it.'

The squad of Russian marines was moving cautiously, their AK 74 assault rifles held at the ready. They kept in single file, each man stepping carefully in the tracks of the one ahead. A young officer led them, he walked stooped over, like a man sensing danger.

As they came to the fringe of a clump of firs he signalled a halt, and took out his binoculars to examine the ground ahead. Twice he swept it, then came back to focus on the network of tracks around the small collection of houses in the distance. He beckoned to his radio-man, and took the handset.

His mouth opened to speak as he pressed the transmit switch, and stayed open as a figure rose up from out of the ground and plunged a knife through the layers of clothing swaddling his neck to cut his windpipe.

The fight was short and vicious, with Hyde's men having the supreme advantage of surprise. Dooley threw himself on three marines, finishing one with the first swing of a length of timber before pain seared his wounded shoulder as he went for a second blow and a Russian ducked in beneath his guard. There was just time for Dooley to divert the wildly wielded club to parry the knife thrust, and then the pair were upon him and he was having to roll and kick to avoid the stabs and blows aimed at his face and chest.

Sweeping aside a rifle butt jabbing at his face, Dooley brought up his studded left boot. Thick clothing prevented the crushing impact doing the intended damage to the Russian's crotch, but it still had sufficient force to hurl him back, and for the moment left Dooley free to concentrate on the marine with the knife.

There was no sound. The fight was going on in complete silence. Even the dead made no noise as they fell, the snow cushioning their fall.

Hyde grabbed a Russian who had a stranglehold on Andrea. Her knife could make no impression on the man's thickly quilted jacket front and sleeves, and with her shorter arms she could not reach his face. Going for the eyes, Hyde missed and felt his fingers slide into the marine's nostrils. Knowing the excruciating pain it would cause he pulled back hard, and the hands locked about the girl's throat were suddenly released.

Blood smothered the sergeant's hand and wrist and showered on Andrea as the flesh split. Reeling at the agony and interested only in escaping the fingers clawing his face, the Russian never saw, and made no move to ward off, the underarm stab that Andrea delivered to his groin.

Bulging eyes stared down at Dooley as he tightened his iron grip on the Russian's face. Foam and spittle bubbled in the back of the man's throat and his struggles grew weaker. Another face appeared over him, looking at him from behind a Makarov pistol. Face and pistol were whirled from sight in a shower of brains and blood at the impact of a close-range burst of automatic fire.

Pushing the dead marine aside, Dooley clambered to his feet. Littering the snow were eight Russian corpses and as many rifles. Between them spots and daubs of blood coloured the white ground, linking them and charting the brief course of the battle.

'I said no bloody noise, no shooting.' Hyde jabbed Ripper in the chest with the tip of the rifle he had wrenched from him. 'What's the bloody use of tackling them with knives and fists if you're going to bang away with this ruddy thing just as we're finishing? Here, take it.' He slung the weapon back at the American. 'Someone will have heard that, we'd better get ready for more visitors.'

'Are we setting up here?' Ripper looked around as the others started to hack at the frozen ground. 'Ain't we going to move a ways from these here cadavers?'

'Don't be sodding stupid.' Libby drove the tip of his entrenching tool into the ground, levering up a saucer-shaped scab of turf and ice-bound soil. 'In a bit these stiffs are going to be just that. They'll make nice ramparts for slit-trenches. They won't stop bullets, but fragments will be slowed down, and a few less feet per second can make all the difference between a flesh wound and losing your head, literally. Now dig.'

'You not searching these then?' Burke shoved a corpse past Dooley with his feet, kicking it into place on the edge of his excavation.

'I got the insignia off the officer, that's the only thing any of this lot will have that's worth taking. Who ever heard of a well-off Ruskie grunt. These stupid shits only got two-hundred-fifty bucks a year. If they'd been the sort who could make a profit, they wouldn't have been here, they'd have been enjoying some cushy number back in Moscow.'

Clarence wasn't happy with an order from Sergeant Hyde. 'It's a waste.'

'It is not a bloody waste. Those special slugs of yours are the only things we've got that will go through armour.'

'They're for tackling body armour, not main battle tanks. Was it a pair of T72s you said the Ruskies had brought ashore? There is no way my bullets can punch through that much plate. It's inches thick in the front, and at the sides they've those side-skirts. The best I shall be able to do is drill holes in that. It's hopeless, absolutely hopeless.'

'And I'm telling you it isn't. Those tanks have been prepared for winter service, and you know how much practice the Ruskies have had at that. Well, they've removed the side-skirts, I suppose to stop snow packing between them and the tracks. If you can stay hidden until they're within fifty feet, you should be able to put a round into them. Now get out to that position on the flank.'

From where they were digging in Hyde could see the sea. It was a good position. They had a field of fire that covered every approach to the house, and the nearest of the launcher sites, a few hundred yards behind them among a dense thicket of evergreens. Again his gaze went to the sea. The ice was increasingly reaching further and further from the shore, growing rapidly by welding on any floes that brushed against it. He couldn't see the *Rogov* itself, but towards the north of the island a tall thick pillar of black smoke rose to be lost from sight in the unnatural-coloured sky. It drove straight into it, without tainting the glowing pallor, as though a hole had opened to receive it. Occasionally he heard a distant rumble as further explosions rocked the ship. It probably wouldn't stay afloat for much longer; there had to be a limit to what the much-repaired hull could take.

'Think we did much damage to those warships, Sarge?' Burke had failed to find an excuse for stopping work for a moment, and now struck up a conversation with his NCO in the hope of inventing one.

'Enough to have scared the shit out of their admiral, I

138

should imagine. The poor sod must have thought he had a safe run until he left Swedish waters. By now he won't know what to bloody do. He can't turn back, he hasn't got the room to manoeuvre without taking his ships into open water, and our subs and mines will be waiting for him there. And the bastard doesn't even know if he can take a swipe at us or not. If he does and the Swedes kick up a stink, then muck will fall on him from a great height. As I will on you if you don't get digging.'

Regretting that the ruse had not worked for longer, Burke resumed his excavations. Frost had bound the root-woven earth together to give it a granite-like consistency. His entrenching tool had to be lifted high and driven in repeatedly before a decent size lump could be hefted on to the parapet. He noticed Dooley taking rests at frequent intervals, trying to conceal a grimace at every effort. 'What's the matter? Has the big hard man got cramp?'

'Shut it. If that hole of yours were ever likely to be deep enough, I'd bury you in it. As it is, you open your trap again and I'll likely turn you inside out and bury you in your own mouth. It's big enough.' With pile-driver force, Dooley sent the blade of his shovel into the soil, until it was hidden by the ice-bound earth. He paid dearly for the gesture, feeling the blood ooze again from his punctured shoulder.

'That'll have to do. Everyone under cover.' Between attempts with cold hands to pile the fruits of his labours on the edge of his slit-trench, Hyde caught a glimpse of movement among distant trees. Waiting a moment to see that the others had gone to ground, he got down himself. It was probably a delusion, but huddled into the all too shallow hole, he felt warmer. After carefully cutting a vee-shaped cleft in the ragged parapet he looked again. There could be no doubt about it, there was the main body of the Russian patrol, perhaps another forty men. It wasn't their loping progress that had first caught his attention. Trees were falling, being toppled and crushed by the advancing bulk of a crudely whitewashed T72.

Even before he could see the details of its raked frontal armour and turret, Hyde had calculated its course. As the tank cleared the tree line, the Soviet marines fanned out behind it, facing him across the half mile of bleak open ground, and started purposefully forward.

THIRTEEN

'Well it had to turn up sooner or later. The rumours have been doing the rounds long enough.' The third battle group showed bright and clear on Cline's screen. Several of the traces were as large as the biggest they had already seen, but one in particular stood out, dwarfing them and shaming the other blips that swarmed about it.

'Seventy thousand tons. The pride of the Russian fleet.' Revell couldn't take his eyes off the image. 'It's just got to be the *Admiral Serget Gorshkov,* that carrier's the biggest hull ever launched from the Leningrad yards. Hell, it's even bigger than anything the Commies have ever laid down at Nikolayev on the Black Sea. York, I want to know if it's operating aircraft, rotary or fixed-wing.'

'I'm already monitoring it, Major, and it's not, but someone is. I've got what sounds like a Swedish fighter controller, seems our neutrals have heard the fireworks going off in their back yard. I can't tell what they're yacking about, sounds like the Swedish chef out of the Muppets, but I'm betting the sky gets rather full in the next couple of minutes.'

'It is already.' Manually activating the automatic IFF interrogator, Cline double-checked the Identification-Friend-or-Foe system. 'And the pair of birds coming our way aren't ours, and they aren't Russian. He could be right.'

'Of course I'm fucking right. Only a genious like me would have checked that channel.' Unable to resist, despite his confidence, York leant over to see his interpretation of the radio-intercept confirmed by two fast-moving traces on the air-watch radar.

'Our fellow islanders have seen them too, they are getting excited.' Over his headphones, Boris could hear the commander of the Russian anti-aircraft missile batteries on the island desperately trying to establish whether or not he could, or should, engage the fast approaching targets. 'In the Red Army it is always the same. Without a specific order to follow, a Soviet officer is terrified of doing the wrong thing, afraid to use initiative.'

'I hear small-arms.' Fraser paused and listened, as he attended to the Swedish woman. His words received immediate attention, and the room was suddenly quiet.

It was unmistakable. The cold, still, air brought the sound of fighting into the room. Revell could discern the brurring chatter of machine guns, the occasional crack of single shots and, more worrying, the sharp smart crash of cannon fire. 'Warn the gunners at the launch sites that the Ruskies are inside the perimeter. And I want the Lance ready to go on a ten-second countdown.'

This was it. Now he felt the sensations that tied Dooley in knots before a fight. Total surprise and confusion among the Russian land and naval forces had kept them safe so far, but now that slight edge was gone. Having shown their hand, they could expect the pressure to build up fast. They would have to do as much damage as they could before the Soviets hit back hard. The marine infantry attack was just the start, the Russian elite troops were, to the barrage that was inevitably coming, what the first loose flake of ice was to an avalanche.

'Major.' York found frequency after frequency jammed with traffic, much of it in code, but a lot of it in clear, as he tapped into the third battle group's ship-to-ship and fire-control communications. 'They're getting ready to chuck hardware, I'm sure of it.'

'How long before the *Gorshkov* is in range?'

'Ten minutes at present course and speed, but some of the escorts are really piling it on. We can have a go at some of them inside five.'

'Hold your fire, Bombardier. Forget the secondary targets, we're waiting for a chance at the jackpot.'

'Think we'll still be around to collect, Major?'

Revell didn't answer York's question. None of the men would have been likely to believe an instant and positive 'yes', and nothing else would have done any good. Already they had done more, much more, than Ol' Foul Mouth or any of the brass had probably expected them to. But even if they'd wanted to, there was no way they could cut and run. They had nowhere to go to, the best they could hope for was to survive whatever the Russians, and perhaps the Swedes, threw at them, and hang grimly on to await a pick-up that might never materialise. This, more than any other mission he'd led the unit into, was taking on all the appearances of a one-way trip.

There was a series of smacks against an outside wall. Fraser fumbled with the sacking he was drawing over the woman's face. Doing so uncovered her blackened legs.

'Just spent rounds from Hyde's fight.'

'That's OK, sir.' Fraser tried to control his shaking hands. 'Just as long as we don't get an "over" from that Ruskie tank.' He moved away from the fresh corpse. 'I'll go back to our casualties now.' Had that one not been available, he would have had to fabricate another excuse to leave the control room. His stomach churned, and for a brief instant his bowels had been about to empty. The sweat that broke from his body instantly seemed to turn to pellets of ice. Though he walked carefully and deliberately, his feet tripped on the stairs and he almost fell, as another group of bullets hit the roof and brought down a tile.

'The kid's shit scared.' York didn't bother to check if he was out of hearing before offering the remark.

'Only a head-case wouldn't be.' It was only partly for the youngster's benefit that Revell said it. There were times when the truth needed to be spoken aloud. None of them were there to throw their lives away. Each of them had passed up a hundred opportunities to do just that in the last few months.

No two members of the unit had the same reason for going on, but the reasons they had were strong, and drove them to fight to stay alive just one more day. In the Zone that was the best you could ever hope for, to see the next day, and there were never any guarantees.

Only ten of the Russian marines were still coming on. They moved in a huddled mass, close behind the slowly advancing bulk of the T72. Their fallen comrades dotted the ground they had already covered, almost impossible to discern in their winter clothing against the backdrop of snow, no more than untidy hummocks marring the pristine white coating over the landscape.

Clarence had held his fire, forcing himself to sublimate the nearly overwhelming urge to take aim, and stayed hidden. But even if he was not as yet involved in the fighting, there was still another battle for him to fight. The air he filtered to his lungs through several layers of scarves struck bitterly cold, but he had the measure of it now. He wasn't about to be caught a second time. Willpower was the only weapon he possessed to aid him in the struggle, and it took all he had to help prevent him closing his eyes and giving in.

A long burst from the tank's co-axial machine gun smacked into the ground beside him, two of the rounds ploughing into the enemy corpse that constituted much of his protection. Made brittle by the cold, the body broke under the impacts, falling apart like a china doll. Unchecked by clothing that snapped as easily as sugar-glass, chunks of face and torso were scattered. An eye and a section of cheek and nose came to rest of the back of the sniper's hand. The contact made him feel sick, had his flesh not been separated from the human debris by the thickness of his gloves he would have vomited. As it was, he flicked his wrist, not watching to see what new resting place the flesh found.

144

He cradled his head, flattening himself into his excavation as the tank fired its main armament. Flame and noise and red-hot fragments lashed the trees behind him, and as that died away it was followed by a burst of automatic fire.

Another of the Russian infantry fell, picked off by a single shot as the jostling of his companions forced him fractionally beyond the shielding steel.

A hundred yards. Clarence chambered the first of the two special bullets he'd taken from the lead-lined container. Seventy-five. He laid the barrel gently in the notch he'd carved in the parapet, and aimed over open sights at the T72. It wasn't a side-on shot, the bullet would impact at an angle of about forty degrees: that increased the thickness of metal it would have to penetrate.

The tank's cannon roared again and sent another shell over their heads. Once more it was the unoffending trees that took the extreme punishment. Far from helping its crew pinpoint their position, the sledgehammer tactics only served to conceal the squad more, adding to the eye-confusing litter of debris about them as smouldering bark and lengths of shattered timber rained down.

Fifty yards. Clarence waited. Forty. Clouds of smoke billowed high above the tank, the multiple exhaust pipes emitting the beat of the big V12 diesel.

A pencil-slim spurt of white and blue flame from the side of the tank's hull, dead centre, just below the top run of track, was the only and unspectacular evidence of the lead-sheathed round's place of impact. Clarence chambered the second bullet and sighted once more, but it wasn't needed.

With its engine screaming at maximum revs, the tank's left track locked and it spun through a half-turn before lurching to a stop as its motor cut.

Suddenly deprived of their mobile cover, the marines hesitated a moment. That cost two more of them their lives as Hyde and the rest of the squad let fly with every weapon. The survivors fell back, firing off hesitant ill-aimed bursts, then turned and began to run.

Standing up and taking her time, Andrea put the last of

them down, her M16's magazine emptying as their final cries echoed back.

There was no smoke or flame coming from the tank, it just sat there, silent and immobile. Libby glanced at it frequently as he worked to deepen his slit-trench. Just as he looked up to check it once more, he saw the distinctive flame-tails of missiles rising from the north of the island. He pointed them out to Sergeant Hyde.

'Could be SAMs, nothing to do with us anyway. Probably some Commie wetting himself and short-circuiting a firing switch.' Hyde grabbed Andrea's rifle, and prevented her from sending a second burst at a wounded Russian who was attempting to crawl away. 'Don't waste ammo. That bugger has got mates who'll be along soon. He won't be taking any more part in the scrap. Let him go, save your bullets for Commies who can hit back.'

A single shot ploughed into the ground between the NCO and the girl, and Hyde made no fresh attempt to stop her when she fired on the casualty they'd spared, and who now supported himself against a tree, aiming with a clumsily held AK74.

Hit by several bullets the Russian threw up his arms and fell backwards. A spurt of flame rose from his body as the contents of an ammunition pouch ignited. Cartridges in the broken magazines began to cook-off, and the corpse jerked with each volley.

'Stupid sod.' Libby went back to his digging.

'Maybe he was trying for a medal.' Through borrowed binoculars Ripper watched the burning corpse jump and twitch. Some of the rounds were going into the body and smashing what wasn't already being consumed by the flames.

'More likely the poor shit was scared of going back and reporting failure. Either he was deliberately committing suicide, or he was using up the last of his ammo to make his story more convincing . . .'

'Or maybe he was a party member,' Dooley added to Hyde's speculations.

'Could be.' Surfacing from the pit he'd made, Burke

146

lodged the blade of his shovel between the upper thighs of a Russian corpse. 'Could well be. Those bleeding card carriers take the cake. Me, I don't reckon any Ruskies, but those real Commies, the party members, nastiest lot of fuckers you'll ever meet. If they hadn't started this bloody war we'd have had to do something about them some day.'

'Here's your chance to do something about them today.' Jumping back into his trench, Hyde tried to count the number of enemy troops pouring from the far woods. He couldn't, there were too many . . . hundreds, and another tank. And this time the Russians were using their classic tactics. As armour and infantry charged, showing none of the slow-paced caution displayed by the earlier patrol, 120mm mortar shells began to fall.

There were no individual ranging shots. The first salvo of five shells fell a hundred yards short, the second, fifty. Hyde ducked down in his trench, clamped his hands over the welded flesh of what had been his ears, and waited for the battery to zero in on his squad's position.

'I couldn't track the SAMs, not with this equipment, but one of those planes is gone from the screen, and there's nothing else to account for it.'

Revell had to accept the bombardier's explanation of the Swedish aircraft's disappearance. The Russians must have gone mad, or if they hadn't, then a battery commander had. Perhaps the Swedes might put up with having one of the islands scorched and battered, and their coastline littered with wrecked shipping; but there was no way they'd shrug off the deliberate destruction of one of their fighters.

'Those three ships left behind by the second battle group are moving.'

'Forget them. Do we have the *Gorshkov* in range yet?' Pacing didn't bring the moment nearer any faster, but it gave Revell something to do. He almost tripped over the woman's body, catching his foot in the sacking draping

147

her, so that it moved and revealed her staring face, spotted with the first marks of frostbite. Even had she survived the wound Ripper had inflicted, she would have almost certainly have lost her legs, and parts of other extremities.

'She's slowed a lot, must be jamming like mad, but if I've picked the right image from among the ghosts on this screen then we can have a go any time.'

'Tell the gunners we're going for broke. Every tube at the carrier. We'll give the Ruskie admiral thirty seconds after we open up. If the crud hasn't retaliated against Swedish territory by then, commence count-down on the Lance. You can use all the remaining decoys this time, York. After this we shan't be needing any more.'

Revell would have given everything to be able to tap, understand and absorb the deluge of radio traffic between the carrier and Moscow, and between the radar-direction, fire-control and reload crews aboard each vessel. That would have told him if something would be coming their way, and when, and how much – but maybe it was better not to know. Only the need to keep Sweden neutral as long as possible had prevented the battle group from wiping the island off the map. The fact that there were Russians on it meant nothing. A single battalion of Soviet marines and their equipment was worth less than nothing in the eyes of the High Command in the Kremlin, when balanced against a vitally needed fleet, and a ship that carried the prestige of the whole country.

There was some small consolation for Revell in knowing that, at the short and still closing range between the island and the battle group, some of the warship's heavier missile armament would be less than effective. Designed to operate against targets fifty or more miles away, it would be almost impossible for the ship's radar to gather and set the missiles towards the island, when their sonic or high subsonic speeds would put them over the dot of land even before the first course correction following launch could be transmitted.

But it was only a very small consolation. Those powerful vessels each had a secondary armament of missiles and conventional weapons capable of delivering a torrent of explosive on to any target, at any distance. Certainly more than enough to saturate the two or three square miles of the island several times over.

The surface radar screen put everything into perspective. To the north, the tail-end of the second battle group, the stragglers whose speed or control or both had been affected by the attack. Nearer the island, the three slow-moving dots of the crippled vessels trying desperately to get out of the path of the approaching carrier and escort, and closer still the slowly fading blip that was the sinking *Ivan Rogov*. But it was the third battle group on which Revell concentrated all his attention.

Aboard those ships, radar operators would be scrutinising their own screens, watching for the first signs of a third attack. The admiral responsible for the carrier group would be on the bridge of the *Gorshkov*, snatching every signal that came in, and dictating an endless stream of his own as he tried to get permission from Moscow to hit back if his precious ship came in for the same treatment that had been meted out to the first and second battle groups.

'Waiting for the word, Major.' Cline was constantly updating the carrier's position on the data links, and doing everything he could to confirm that the particular blip he had chosen was indeed the *Gorshkov* and not a decoy transmission.

'They're not going to like us doing it to them again.' York noticed a slight but perceptible falling off in the quantity of enemy radio traffic. 'I think they've got themselves near enough ready now, Major. The flap's over, now they're just sitting there, waiting, like a bloody great cat for a little weak mouse.'

'Not as weak as all that.' Revell held his fire a moment longer.

The lead escort ships were slowing down as they drew abreast of the island, to make a corridor of defensive fire for the carrier as it passed.

In the silence of the room, Revell could hear mortar

fire, punctuated by the crack of a cannon and the near continuous rattle of machine guns. Hyde too had a fight on his hands, but he had started early. It was time for them to join in.

'Fire.'

FOURTEEN

Above the thunder of the mortar barrage, above the crash and clatter of cannon and automatic fire, Hyde heard the multiple rocket launchers go into action. He had to turn, squirming around in his trench, to watch the projectiles ride their tails of flame into the sky. Their scream blotted every other noise from existence as they leapt upwards in a never ending stream. He couldn't watch them all, the Russian marines were getting close, and he had to turn back to add the puny contribution of his rifle to the pathetic volume that was all his squad could muster against the weapons massed against them.

Soviet infantrymen were falling, many of them, but there were always more to keep the attack pressing forward. The wave of relief Hyde had experienced when the rain of mortar shells suddenly ceased was instantly wiped away by the realisation that it marked the moment for the enemy to close in and finish the unequal battle.

'Take that, you shits.' Determined to use every last round, to sell himself as dear as he could, Hyde sent a burst into a knot of marines advancing ahead of the main body. Four of them went down. He replaced the clip and sighted again. He could see the open mouths of the men who were still advancing, they must be shouting but he couldn't hear them.

A mortar shell fell close, and Hyde felt needles of fire in

his side. This might be his last chance, he took careful aim.

The Russians seemed to dissolve, fall apart. There was a gigantic explosion and bodies and limbs were suddenly flying through the air. A dozen more of the massive detonations followed in quick succession and the attack faltered, stopped, and was destroyed.

The open ground was torn into a bloody moonscape under the pulverising blows. The knocked-out tank disappeared inside a huge fireball, that lifted to reveal no vestige of the machine. Stalled, abandoned by its crew, the second T72 was lifted and thrown thirty yards, all forty-six tons of it, to land upside down in a steaming crater.

As shock wave after shock wave washed over him, Burke clung to the earth. At every blast the hard ground smacked into his face, but he didn't move, preferring its punishment to the consequences of raising his head. Two enormous explosions that erupted almost simultaneously ended the pounding, and after a moment he cautiously looked up.

The scene had been changed beyond all recognition. What had recently been snow-covered ground, swarming with white-clad yelling troops, was now a wasteland of churned and heaped soil, dotted with the gruesome and not always identifiable remains of broken bodies.

A handful of shocked and wounded Russians wandered about the periphery of the area. Now and again one would collapse to become another grisly ornament on hell's landscape. Dark red flame licked from a trackless tank upside down in a crater.

'That wasn't our stuff, that was from the ships. The Ruskies have clobbered their own ruddy men.' Libby emerged from the ground, to join the others who were looking in awe at the results of the bombardment.

Even Andrea could only stare, for once not thinking to aim at the enemy wounded tottering away between what was left of the trees.

Several pillars of black smoke were rising from the

north of the island accompanied by the sound of ammunition burning, and an occasional fountain of white fire laced with red and green tracer.

'I sure as hell don't know why those guys are going that way, there just ain't nothing left for them to go back to.' Ripper half-lifted his rifle to his shoulder to take a shot, but lowered it again.

'The state those poor buggers are in, they don't know where they're going.' Hyde could feel the slivers of metal in his side as he moved the muscles in which they were embedded. He'd had worse, much worse. Most of the others were flecked with blood, and Dooley had a long cut across one cheek. He kept fingering it, and asking Ripper if it looked like it'd leave a scar, his tone suggested that he was hoping it would. 'Right, back to the house. We're not needed here any more. The Russian navy had done our work for us.'

'Obliging blokes, aren't they?' Libby shouldered his rifle. He was eager to get back within the shelter of those four walls. It might lack creature comforts, but the house was a better place to wait for their pick-up than out here. Hell, he was getting fond of the place. In his mind's eye he'd been working on various ideas of how to turn it into a nice home for him and Helga. Now he was almost looking forward to spending a few more hours there.

As he took his first step towards it, the whole length of the village erupted. Libby stopped, seeking the house through the dust and smoke and flying snow. It was still there, still safe.

Two more of the big missiles struck, bracketing the house and hiding it inside a storm of giant debris. Slowly at first, then faster, Libby began to run towards the village. Briefly he saw the house again; a wall had gone, the roof, much of the upper floor, then another round plunged down and flame hid it once more.

Fraser was smothered in blood. He half-staggered, half-fell over the mangled tangle of bodies partially blocking the stairs.

Peering past the medic, Revell could make out daylight, or as much as could be seen through the thick dust and smoke. The whole of the top of the house had gone. Two white bars from his eyes to the corners of his mouth had been inscribed on the youngster's face as his tears washed he blood and dirt from their tracks. Revell sat him down in York's chair, first pushing the radio-man's headless body aside.

'Where is it, where is it?' Cline scrambled about on the floor. He picked up a scrap of paper, then a second. 'It's all gone, my notes, all gone.'

'Did we get the *Gorshkov?*' Using his sleeve Revell wiped Fraser's face, finding no injury.

'I don't know. They were jamming, more than I've ever seen. Have you seen the rest of my notebook?' Glass broke under his hands but Cline didn't notice. There was no more to be found. 'Lousy bloody Russians.' As though doing it for the first time, he continually turned the two scraps over and over in his hand. They were blank pages from the back of the book. 'Should have taken more notes, filled it, then there'd be something on these.'

'Is there anything left of the radio?'

'No, Major.' Boris pushed the equipment's remains on to the floor. 'Everything is broken, everything.' Strips of clean bandage bound around his wrist made a stark contrast to the flame-singed remnants of his jacket. He pulled the remains together, but there was nothing to fasten it with, and little enough left to fasten. With difficulty, he began to strip the blood-soaked anorak off York's body.

It was too much for Fraser, to see the decapitated corpse lolling back and forth as Boris clumsily worked at it with his one good hand. The medic drew his hood around his face and closed the opening with his hands, clenching them tight until the knuckles were pure white.

There was a fire at the back of the house, and other buildings nearby, what was left of them, were also beginning to burn. They might as well leave now, they'd be forced to soon enough anyway. There was nothing worth gathering up, Revell knew that without looking. He guided Fraser, and pushed Cline, ahead of him. Outside, the row of bodies had gone and little of what had previously been surrounding the house was still in place. The very paths had been torn up or buried, and deep craters dictated a zig-zag path as they moved away. Smoke stung his eyes, and he felt the heat of the flames consuming the heaps of rubble. It was a strange sensation that warmth, almost alien, like a brief recollection of a half-forgotten memory.

The numbing shock of the barrage was slow to wear off, Revell felt it clouding his mind, struggled to shake free of it. For no obvious reason, perhaps only due to blind instinct, he turned towards the shore.

Someone was shouting, running towards him. The major let go of Fraser, and reached for his 12-gauge assault rifle. He had hung on to it through everything, but now as he unslung it, it felt unfamiliar. As he brought it up to fire at the approaching figure, he realised how badly damaged it was. Deep inside, his mind sluggishly recognised the irony. The weapon was like him, intact but incapable of functioning properly. As he slowly examined it, fire-scarred hands carefully took it from his grasp.

There was no expression on Hyde's face, there never could be, but Revell sensed the sergeant's concern. 'I'm OK, just a bit scrambled; take charge, will you.' Only distantly did he hear Hyde bark a string of orders. Faces around him were indistinct, he just wanted to get away, be by himself, but there was something else he had to do first, something he had to tell the NCO. The thought crept through the darkness in his head, trying to surface. 'Get the men over to the shore, the cabin. If anyone comes to pick us up, that's where they'll look first.'

'That's a fucking great "if".' Dooley took the major's arm, and began to lead him, as he had earlier lead Fraser.

Revell didn't resist. It was good to temporarily relinquish the responsibility of choosing what route to take. His legs moved mechanically and kept moving, even when his mind switched off completely.

'The captain says he'll send the signal when we surface.'
Hyde settled himself on the floor of the submarine's
control room beside the major.

Awareness was coming back to Revell, but it was a slow
process, and he needed moments to form thoughts that
would normally be instantaneous. 'Is there any word
about the Russian ships?'

'Not a lot, but the captain says that's good. They should
have popped up in the North Sea by now, but they
haven't. The Swedes are kicking up bloody hell. Doesn't
matter that the barrage destroyed the Lance, seems some
of the Russian "overs" went on to clobber seven sorts of
brickdust out of the mainland. Accusations and counter-
accusations are flying all over. Probably won't come to a
fight, but suddenly the Swedes aren't friends with
Moscow. Oh yes, one of their main complaints is about a
ruddy great aircraft carrier that's gone aground off Goth-
enburg. Thought you'd like to know that.'

Little by little, Fraser had edged out from the self-
imposed internal exile of his hood. He looked around the
shining clean control and crew-filled room. This was a
better way to go to war, isolated at a distance from the
death and ugliness. A crewman handed him a large mug of
soup and he clasped his hands about it. The submariner
was about his own age, and Fraser felt he could talk to
him.

'I've never been in a sub before, what sort is it?'

'Oberon class, *HMS Onyx*. She's a hunter-killer.'

Fraser put the soup back on the tray, pulled his hood
tight across his face, and hid from the war.

TIGER
by James Rouch

They were behind enemy lines as the battle for
Normandy raged around them; their radio was useless;
and between them and their base lay the deadliest
weapon of the entire German army — a lone Tiger tank.

The Tiger Mark I — the pride of the mighty Panzer
divisions; the scourge of the Allied forces. To fight
against one was a nightmare; to fight against one and
survive was close to a miracle.

Each man in Sergeant Ellis's patrol had his own reason
for hating them. Now they had their chance for revenge.
Six men against a monstrous machine of death, and all
the exits were blocked . . .

NEW ENGLISH LIBRARY

THE WAR MACHINES
by James Rouch

'In the machines those boffins keep bodging up it's more like bloody suicide. And as if it's not bad enough going to war in their death-traps, in this god-forsaken hell-hole of a desert, we have to have Hoskins, the only sergeant in the war who actually enjoys being shot at — and takes a sadistic pleasure in sharing the experience with his less heroic subordinates. That crazy bastard's antics are more terrifying than the entire German Army . . .

How Frank Davies and his mates coped with everything the enemy and their superiors threw at them, and how they hit back, makes an explosive novel of World War 2.

NEW ENGLISH LIBRARY

GATEWAY TO HELL
by James Rouch

Monte Cassino, impregnable core of the German
defences, looming over the most savage battlefield in
Italy, stands between the advancing Allies and their goal.

Lieutenant Saville's Assault Engineers and their escort
from the crack New Zealand 2nd Division are ordered to
destroy a key position in the shadow of the Monastery.

None of them can foresee the ferocity of the enemy's
attempt to obstruct them. Cut off, forced to shelter
behind the corpses of their comrades, they face the
fanatical paratroops of the Hermann Goering Division.

With the Paras, pitting his wits against Saville and
staking his life on success, is Hauptmann Wolff, the
engineer who designed the strong-point. It is a struggle
neither can afford to lose. because whoever holds the
Fuehrer Emplacement controls the road to Rome — and
the armies are poised for battle.

NEW ENGLISH LIBRARY

NEL BESTSELLERS

T037061	BLOOD AND MONEY	*Thomas Thompson*	£1.50
T045692	THE BLACK HOLE	*Alan Dean Foster*	95p
T049817	MEMORIES OF ANOTHER DAY	*Harold Robbins*	£1.95
T049701	THE DARK	*James Herbert*	£1.50
T045528	THE STAND	*Stephen King*	£1.75
T065475	I BOUGHT A MOUNTAIN	*Thomas Firbank*	£1.50
T050203	IN THE TEETH OF THE EVIDENCE	*Dorothy L. Sayers*	£1.25
T050777	STRANGER IN A STRANGE LAND	*Robert Heinlein*	£1.75
T050807	79 PARK AVENUE	*Harold Robbins*	£1.75
T042308	DUNE	*Frank Herbert*	£1.50
T045137	THE MOON IS A HARSH MISTRESS	*Robert Heinlein*	£1.25
T050149	THE INHERITORS	*Harold Robbins*	£1.75
T049620	RICH MAN, POOR MAN	*Irwin Shaw*	£1.60
T046710	EDGE 36: TOWN ON TRIAL	*George G. Gilman*	£1.00
T037541	DEVIL'S GUARD	*Robert Elford*	£1.25
T050629	THE RATS	*James Herbert*	£1.25
T050874	CARRIE	*Stephen King*	£1.50
T050610	THE FOG	*James Herbert*	£1.25
T041867	THE MIXED BLESSING	*Helen Van Slyke*	£1.50
T038629	THIN AIR	*Simpson & Burger*	95p
T038602	THE APOCALYPSE	*Jeffrey Konvitz*	95p
T046850	WEB OF EVERYWHERE	*John Brunner*	85p

NEL P.O. BOX 11, FALMOUTH TR10 9EN, CORNWALL

Postage charge:

U.K. Customers. Please allow 40p for the first book, 18p for the second book, 13p for each additional book ordered, to a maximum charge of £1.49, in addition to cover price.

B.F.P.O. & Eire. Please allow 40p for the first book, 18p for the second book, 13p per copy for the next 7 books, thereafter 7p per book, in addition to cover price.

Overseas Customers. Please allow 60p for the first book plus 18p per copy for each additional book, in addition to cover price.

Please send cheque or postal order (no currency).

Name ....

Address ....

....

Title ....

While every effort is made to keep prices steady, it is sometimes necessary to increase prices at short notice. New English Library reserve the right to show on covers and charge new retail prices which may differ from those advertised in the text or elsewhere.(5)